A Street King's Dream 2

By: EL Griffin

D1550845

Imani

"What the fuck Demont!? You don't have to do this!" I screamed at him from the passenger seat of his car.

The same car I used to drive around in like I was a part of a happy family. Not having a damn clue who this nigga really was. But now I knew and I wanted no parts. To make it so bad, Demont was even more fucked up than I thought. He was out of his mind crazy on some kidnapping shit and looking like a straight junkie.

"Shut the fuck up! Your hoe ass 'bout to wake my daughter up and shit. The fuck you think was gon' happen Imani? That I was gon' let you leave me? That shit's dead. I told you, you're mine. Your ass ain't goin' no fucking where. You hear me?" He reached over, gripped my chin hard. Then slapped the shit out of me. So hard my head hit the door window.

It hurt like hell and brought tears to my eyes, but the impact knocked some damn sense into my ass too. And at that point I stopped fucking talking. Not saying another word to this lame ass nigga. But not because of the pain in my head. It was only for the sake of Amyra. I didn't want her to witness any of this shit. And I didn't want Demont to do some more stupid shit that might harm her.

I swear I would've taken a swing at his ass if I could. But Demont duct taped my hands behind my back after forcing me at gunpoint to put Amyra in the backseat. Going to the extreme. He wrapped

5

them tight as hell around my back, damn near using the whole role of tape. Luckily Amyra was asleep as soon as I set her down in the back so she didn't have to see none of the shit.

Demont was smart with it, because I would have busted his face wide open the second I got a chance otherwise. Especially now that the car was stopped and parked in his mother's driveway like shit was good. Pulling in as if I was a willing participant in this kidnapping. Which wasn't the case at all!

Out of all the places this nigga could've brought us, he chose his momma's house. It wasn't far away or nothing. Right here in the same town less than 30 minutes from my house. I really wondered what his end game was. What did he hope to accomplish by bringing us here? He must have really lost his damn mind if he thought shit was gonna be sweet.

Demont went into the backseat, got Amyra out and took her inside the house. I could have left. But there was no fucking way I was leaving without my daughter.

A few minutes later he came back and opened my door up. And I was ready for his ass. As soon as he reached for my arm, I stood up fast getting up out of the car. Then stomped down hard as hell on his foot. I screamed at the top of my lungs while he was bent over and stumbling around. Hoping somebody would do something. Or call the police. As much as I hated them right now I needed to get me and my daughter the fuck away from this nigga. Him being high as hell played to my advantage for the moment.

"HELP!!!! HELP!!!! HELP!!!!!" My voice rang out across the dark streets of the North Side where we were. So loud there was an echo.

There weren't many people out but enough that you would think some damn body would try and do something. But nope, not a single person did more than turn their head my way. See me tied up under the dim light of one of the street lamps. Then they all looked away again, minding their own damn business. When you really needed help mothafuckas turned the other cheek. Literally.

Demont stood up and wrapped both his hands around my neck. Tightening his grip with that same crazy ass look from earlier. Cutting off my air supply. And I couldn't even reach up to try and stop him. His ass was really trying to kill me. Right here in the middle of the night in his momma's driveway. My thoughts went to my daughter. Then to Khalil. I felt tears at the corners of my eyes as my lungs started straining, with no air coming in. I didn't want to go out like this. *Please God protect my daughter*, I thought silently.

Khalil (King)

Coup laid on the fucking hospital bed. Bleeding through the gauzes and shit the doctors pressed against his chest. I looked in through the window watching as they worked on him. Shit was fucked up. This was the room they wheeled him into after I carried his lifeless body into the emergency room.

Most niggas would've dropped their homeboy off and came back to check after shit cooled down. But I wasn't most niggas and this was my family. Our team was solid, but this was my fucking brother's life we were talking about. That cousin and partna shit didn't even explain our bond on some real shit. So I was staying until I got Brandi up here. Even if that meant dealing with the police. That's why I hit her line as soon as they rolled out the bed for me to lay his body on when I came in. I didn't have time to talk and explain shit though, so I sent a text instead. Just telling her to come up to the hospital and ask for Coup.

Shit was all the way bad right now. First Imani was missing and then Coup's car was shot up. This shit wasn't a fucking coincidence either. It was clear as fucking day that those niggas across town made their fucking move. And the fucked up part was as big as our shit was getting we weren't built to handle the pressure off top. Right now we were like sitting ducks out here. And that's why this bullshit could happen in the first place.

8

"OH MY GOD! WHAT HAPPENED? IS HE OKAY?" Brandi's voice made her presence known before I saw her.

She screamed and went to rush in the door without stopping to wait and get an answer from me. I reached out and grabbed her arm, catching her before she got her ass kicked out of the damn hospital. I needed her to be solid and hold shit down. Whether she was a real bitch or not was about to show. Times like these a person's true colors showed.

"Whoa, Whoa. Chill out sis. Calm the fuck down." I kept my voice steady but stern.

After pausing, I looked her dead in the eyes. To get her to calm down like I said and hold herself together. She needed to hold shit down for her nigga right now. She shook her head "yes", taking my words for what they were. Then wiped away the tears and kept her mouth shut.

I didn't give a fuck how I came off. There wasn't any of that soft shit right now. I couldn't shield her from this bullshit. And time was still fucking ticking on finding her best friend as it was.

"They're working on him now. He took a slug to the chest. And I need you to hold shit down here and keep yo' shit together shorty. Coup needs you now. I gotta go take care of some things."

Brandi looked like she wanted to ask more questions. But after another pause still standing facing me, I saw her get her fucking head on straight. And right then from her expression I knew she was a real one. That shit was hard to come by

9

and Coup needed a bitch like that in his corner. We all did out here.

She nodded, then turned back around, like I wasn't even fucking standing there anymore and went back to the door. Standing, watching through the hospital door window. Taking my spot.

I did the same shit, turning around and walking my ass back out the way I came in. My thoughts going back to finding Imani.

I didn't have a fucking choice at this point but to involve some of the other niggas on our team. I guess it was time to see if they had a fucking backbone. Beyond the street shit, this had to do with family.

I hit up our top lieutenant and told him to meet up with his team over at our spot. The one we named "yellow", since "central" was hot as a mothafucka right now. All our spots were shut down for the night now and our team was on standby. Waiting for word on the next move. They better be ready to fucking slide after the bold face shit those niggas pulled coming against us.

We wouldn't back down from a mothafuckin' thing. And it was time to let them know that shit. At the same time, I had to think about Imani. There was no way I was going in blind and jeopardizing her life. We couldn't go to their side, start spraying and end up hitting her. That wasn't a fucking option. Not without knowing if she was over there.

The wheels in my head were already turning on how to play it. The shit I came up with was gonna be a big ass risk but real niggas took real risks when it came to protecting theirs.

Imani

Demont recovered from me stomping on his foot within seconds and had his hand over my mouth to stop me from screaming. He tightened his other arm around the rest of me. Pulling me towards the back of the house. Not the same way he took Amyra in.

One of my feet caught on the first step up to the backdoor. Causing me to fall forward and land on my face. My nose started pouring down blood immediately and I screamed out, "AHHHH!"

Feeling like my shit was broke. Demont held onto my arm and yanked my ass right back up with his tight grip. My head and body were in the worst pain I'd ever felt, but I kept walking. Staggering in behind the fuck nigga.

He pulled me roughly inside the house behind him. Through the dark kitchen and into a small ass hallway that he led me to. He stopped, reached up and pulled on a string chain I hadn't noticed. It was above his head a foot or so. He pulled down and backed up to let the narrow ass attic steps come down. Then pushed me in front of him. Holding my ass and giving another push so I'd go up. Leaving his hands on me as if he wasn't forcing me here and this shit wasn't fucked up.

I turned around ready to talk shit. But Demont must have been expecting that shit because the second my head was turned, he had the pistol pressed against the small of my back. So I turned the fuck back around and made my way up the steps. Taking them slow since I couldn't see shit. When I made it to the top, I was tempted to stomp this nigga again. This time on the damn head. But Demont still had the gun aimed right at me when I stepped up onto the floor and turned back around.

The attic didn't have enough room for me to stand all the way up. So I had to keep my knees bent and head slanted to the side with the angled ceiling. There was a hanging light turned on which at least let me see what the fuck was up here. As my eyes scanned the small attic I took in my surroundings. Thinking of a way to get out of here. All that was up here was an air mattress and a wood box flipped upside down next to it. With an ash tray and old blunts left in it. The makeshift bed had a blanket tossed on it.

It looked like this nigga had been sleeping up here for a minute from the number of blunts. The shit was weird as hell to me. But I honestly didn't give a fuck about what he had going on to even want to question the shit. All I cared about was getting my ass up out of here and taking my daughter to safety with me.

"Go 'head and lay down baby. You ain't going nowhere." Demont gestured with the gun. Moving his hand towards that direction.

"What you mean lay down? And I'm not going nowhere Demont? Why are you doing this shit? We can sit down and talk like two grown ass people."

"Bitch!" He came closer and slapped the shit out of me for the second time tonight. His hand made direct contact with my skin, making my head snap back. I couldn't even defend myself with my hands wrapped in tape. But I stood my damn ground and glared up at his ass in the dim light. Ready to fuck him up given the opportunity. That's how I was feeling right now. He'd never put his hands on me before. Not ever. But tonight every single damn thing he was doing was some shit he never pulled before. The nigga in front of me was a complete stranger.

I wasn't giving up that easy though. I would just be smarter about getting me and my baby out of this nigga's grasp and out of harms way.

"Okay, Okay. I'm sorry." I changed my tune quick as hell and laid the fuck down.

Adjusting my body to get somewhat fake comfortable on the cold air mattress. It was awkward as hell with my hands behind my back and with my body sore as hell. But it was time to act. I faked the look I gave him next. One that was submissive, hiding the hatred that he caused to come up in me tonight.

"I'm not going anywhere baby. I'm sorry for everything."

"That's all you had to say. Shit!"

"Can you at least undo my hands, so I can lay with you right?"

"I don't know..."

"I mean what can I do with you right next to me? Like I said I'm sorry. I'm not going anywhere. You'll know if I try anything anyway. You got quick reflexes remember?" I added. Playing on the fact he thought he was still that same athlete he used to be.

But I knew he was high as hell and hopefully would pass out. Like he did when he got drunk. He came over to the side of the mattress and used his lighter to burn through the duct tape. I couldn't even lie the heat from the flame hurt, but it meant nothing compared to having my hands free. That was the only way I'd be able to get away from here.

As soon as he pulled the extra tape off, I smiled up at him seductively and then laid down on my side. Arm up under my head and bent using it as a pillow. Demont got on the bed himself and laid up behind me. Spooning me, his body close like we'd spent a hundred nights before. But this time I knew my body was stiff as a damn board. And no amount of faking was changing that shit.

"So what now?" I asked quietly and sweetly.

"Take yo' ass to sleep. I'm tired as fuck. And been missing you next to me. Got a nigga going crazy and shit." I heard his voice getting lower, sounding like he was already about to fall asleep.

But that wasn't my damn luck. Not before he tried feeling me up and down like he was gonna try some shit. And even if I was faking being cool for a minute. I wasn't gonna let this nigga fuck. I'd put up a fight first. I couldn't let his dirty dick inside me. Not ever again.

"I'm on my period." I said quick and louder. Scooting my ass away from feeling his dick pressed against it.

15

He gripped my waist right around my hip with his hand and squeezed. Held still for a second like he was thinking about the shit I said. I waited for something. But nothing came. And within a few minutes his light snoring turned into a loud ass grumble. With his chest moving up and down causing the whole fucking air mattress to move.

I laid perfectly still. Plotting my escape step by step.

When I did get up, I was gonna have to move fast as hell. So I thought over the situation perfectly in my head time after time. Letting Demont fall into an even deeper sleep. He damn sure was on some drugs, pills or something mixed with the liquor I smelled on his breath. Which played to my advantage because his stupid ass really fell asleep like I was in here willingly and not gonna try and escape. I turned my head a little trying to peek back around my shoulder at him. To see where the hell he put the gun.

I couldn't see the box table to see if it was on top. I guess I'd have to see if Demont still had it on him. As risky as it was, I knew I didn't have a choice. So I slid my hand back reaching out on his stomach first. Making contact. I felt his abs and then as calm as I could, moved my hand down some like I was rubbing and asleep myself. Demont scared the fuck out of me when his body moved under my touch. Going from his side to his back all of the sudden. And his snoring stopped. I instantly froze in place. Thinking his ass had woke up. I left my hand right the fuck where it was, just at the top

16

of his belt buckle. This nigga laid down jeans and all right out the streets for the day. He was stupid as hell for real.

I waited again. And thankfully nothing came. He didn't make another move and now that my hand was in contact with him, I felt his breathing become even and steady again. Slow and deep. His snoring had stopped but I was confident he was back in a good ass sleep.

I waited at least another 20 minutes, eyes wide staring at the black wall in front of me counting to sixty over and over. Trying to keep calm and my mind focused.

Finally I slid my hand over to his side, now that it was at his belt and luckily felt the gun handle tucked in the top of his pants. I put my fingers around the handle and tugged gentle at first. But the shit didn't budge. So I took a deep breath, counted to 3 and then in one swift motion took the risk and pulled hard a shell. At the same time, I hopped the fuck up. Like a damn track athlete jumping like a bitch was about to win the high jump. Not even making the touchy ass air mattress move that much for what the hell it was.

I spun around, aimed the gun at Demont. I know I looked like a crazy ass bitch. And at this point that was exactly what this nigga had made me. He still laid perfectly still, knocked out in a deep ass sleep. I moved over towards the drop down stairs that were pulled up. Keeping my body turned to watch Demont the entire time. Walking sideways not turning my back for nothing.

I squatted down and pushed the steps back down. Causing another loud ass noise from them dropping back down, but this nigga was out cold. I don't know how he called himself pulling this shit off for real in the state he was in to begin with. But it worked out in me and Amyra's favor. I stepped down, gaining confidence now. Going faster with every step. Four steps down and I was touching the floor back in the hallway again.

I left the steps how they were and moved through the rest of the house. I was familiar enough with the shit to make my way in the dark. The living room TV was the only light. And it masked the sound of my footsteps. I went into the living room then turned the corner, tucking the gun in the front of my pajama short set. It was an elastic band so it wasn't doing a good ass job of securing it, but I had to think of something so I could grab Amyra.

Rushing ahead, more frantic now. I hurried into the room she slept in and picked her up. My adrenalin pumping. Making everything faster. I didn't think twice or look back once I made it to the front door. Swinging it open. Not giving a fuck that it slammed back shut at this point. I hurried out of the house. Already planning on running. Still carrying a sleeping Amyra to the corner store. Away from these North Side niggas. It was about a half mile to the busiest one. From there I would walk the rest of the way to my mother's place. It was the closest place to go and find safety.

I was out of options at this point. It was the middle of the night. I didn't have a car, cash or clothes for that matter. I luckily convinced Demont to let me put on a pair of slides and kept them on my feet the entire time. So at least I wasn't barefoot. All I could think of was getting to the house before Demont woke up and realized we were gone. I needed to get me and my daughter the hell away from Wilmington. It wasn't safe here anymore. And my so called man was nowhere to be found and couldn't protect me either.

Brandi

Standing at the hospital door, staring in at Coup's lifeless body seemed surreal. I had gone numb. First in shock when I realized why King called me. Damn near losing it for real when I first got here. King talking shit snapped me out of it. And now I was somewhat holding it together. Keeping my feelings pushed down and watching without letting myself think beyond the shit I was seeing.

Then hours passed, coming and going. They moved Coup from the emergency room to the ICU. He wasn't being worked on, but he was in critical condition so I couldn't go in and see him yet. Since it was still touch and go. I couldn't do shit but wait this out and pray. So that's exactly what the hell I did.

I sat down in one of the hard ass double chairs in the corner of the closest waiting room to where he was. It was the middle of the night so at least it was quiet in this part of the hospital. Except for the occasional codes coming over the intercom. Each time, I held my breath hoping not to hear a "code blue" and have the doctors come out and tell me the unthinkable when it came to Coup. Thankfully, that shit never came.

I found myself dozing off, holding my arms inside my shirt's short sleeves. Trying to keep warm in this cold ass place. I hated hospitals. To me it was always some nosy mothafuckas asking too many questions, all the times I had to come here with one of my sisters or brothers. Bringing them up here for different sicknesses or accidents. My mother didn't handle shit good. So I always stepped in and handled the "real" parenting shit for her. The things she was supposed to be doing as our parent. It just wasn't in her.

Next thing I knew I felt the bright rays of sunlight shining on me from the window. Just about blinding me when I finally opened my eyes all the way, remembering where I was. Reaching my hand up to my neck, I tried to rub the stiffness out. I had slept sitting up straight with my neck slumped to the side.

I stood up, looked around trying to figure out where my best bet was to get information. I decided to try at the receptionist desk in the ICU corridor.

"Excuse me. I'm trying to get information on Zaire Jones's condition."

"Well..." The ugly ass nurse started. Coming at me with bullshit.

I thought the old man who had been on duty during the night was good for nothing. But not out of spite. He was just too damn old. But this bitch here was on some petty ass hating shit. I could tell from the smirk and attitude with the way she said, "*well*." It was always jealous ugly bitches that thought their position was more than it was.

I kept my cool though, not showing the aggravation that this bitch was causing. Testing my nerves early as hell while the man I loved... or cared about was touch and go with his fucking life. I

21

corrected my thoughts real quick. Not ready for the "L" word even in my mind.

"Look, I just need to know what room he's in and when the doctor's will be making their rounds."

I was smart enough to know not to try and get this bitch to give me any useful information. The bare minimum was a fucking room number. Since last night the nurse on duty told me they'd be moving Coup after the tests they scheduled. I already knew that I overslept that shit. So as soon as this hoe could give me the answer I was looking for, I'd gladly keep it moving and get out of her way.

"He's in 142. But..."

I didn't wait and listen. Instead, I turned around and walked my ass down the hall. Ignoring whatever else she called herself trying to tell me. I didn't have time to deal with the attitude. And I didn't want to get kicked out for beating the hoe's ass. Then I'd have to get bailed out while my man was laid up. Nope, I'd pass on all that.

I found the room easy enough. The door was mostly closed, cracked only a little. I pushed it open expecting to see Coup alone in his room or maybe with a damn nurse. But most definitely not with the same bitch standing over his bed that was on his porch the other day. After dealing with the receptionist and now seeing this bitch, I couldn't hold my anger back anymore.

"Bitch get the fuck out of here!" I charged at her ass.

Damn near running. Ready to tussle. Since she was bold enough to show her face even after

Coup checked her. She didn't want to listen then. So now I was gonna make her listen.

"Wait! Wait!" She held her hands up waving them in front of her face. "I'm here because I'm supposed to be. I love Zaire and he loves me. We've been together for years. Really, I should be telling you to leave. Who are you again?"

Fuck no, this bitch wasn't trying to flip shit and catch an attitude. When a second ago she was scary as hell. I guess she talked herself up. But she picked the wrong bitch to try. I was just as classy and put together as I wanted to be like her stuck up ass. But best believe that hood shit was in me too. And that was the difference between me and her. And she must not have known who she was fucking with. Not when it came to "Zaire" or me.

I didn't give a fuck who she thought she was to Coup. I heard him tell her that he was with me and for her to kick rocks. So all her words did was piss me off more. Here my man was fighting for his life and she brought this negative ass energy around him. She was an insecure selfish hoe. Anybody who really loved a person would do what was best for them, not themselves.

I pulled my arm back so quick she never saw the shit coming. And my fist landed hard as hell right against her eye. She screamed out. She should've kept those hands up to block her face like she was when I approached. Stupid hoe.

I swear to god, she had tears in her eyes just from that shit, which wasn't anything. I was keeping my composure considering how shit

23

could've gone. I only threw a single punch. I was pregnant after all. I couldn't forget.

Even though I had been planning to get an abortion. That was before. Before last night when every thing changed. Now I wasn't so sure. Hours of uncertainty with whether Coup would pull through or not left my decision about our unborn in the balance as well.

Not wanting to hear this bitch's shrill voice anymore, I snatched her by the elbow and pulled her towards the door. I wasn't wasting another word on her. She gasped but didn't say shit else either. And she didn't have it in her to try and fight back. She was lucky today, because my temper was usually bad as hell. I was proud of myself for not whooping her ass for real.

After pushing her out of the door, I went ahead and closed it back all the way. Not turning around to wait and see if she came back in. I knew she wouldn't. I was shaking mad. I took a few deep breaths, staring straight ahead at Coup laying on the bed. Then walked over to his bedside. Stood close as hell and continued looking down at him.

His face still looked almost perfect to me. His light brown skin was more pale than usual, but otherwise it looked like he was asleep. But I knew better. And the loud ass beeping from the machine didn't let me forget. I ran my hand gently over his jaw.

"I'm sorry bae. I'm here for you now. You can't leave me. Leave us." I put my other hand on my stomach and sat down in the chair beside the bed.

Pulled it closer to Coup's bed and picked up his hand. The one without the IV and heart monitor. I kissed the back of his hand. Feeling his cold clammy skin. But I didn't care. Touching him, being close made me feel useful. Even though there wasn't shit I could do for him other than be by his side for when he woke up. That was exactly what the fuck I was going to do. I'd be here when he woke up. I wasn't giving doubt a foothold. Coup was strong and a fighter.

I leaned my head in and laid it near where I let his hand rest back on the bed. Then closed my eyes. Saying a silent prayer to God for his protection and health to be restored. And then the tears came. That's when I realized Coup really did mean more to me than any other man ever had. And I finally admitted to myself that I loved him.

Imani

I didn't know how long it had been, but it seemed like fucking forever. My feet hurt. My body was sore all over. My face and arms. Everywhere that nigga touched hurt and I knew the bruises would show up tomorrow. But what choice did I have.

Here I was walking across town in the middle of the damn night. Without real clothes, no money, pocketbook, cell phone, car, not a damn thing. With my two-year-old daughter sleeping heavy as hell in my arms. I kept walking though. Trying not to be paranoid as hell. Thinking Demont would roll up on us and this shit would've all been for nothing.

But as soon as I spotted the entrance to my mother's apartment complex I sped up as fast as I could with Amyra in my arms. Thank God I made it. I was ready to fall over any second. It's true that a mother's strength did what needed to be done. But by now my adrenalin was wearing off and all I wanted was comfort and a safe place for a minute. My mind had been racing and paranoid as fuck the whole walk. My momma's place was on the opposite side of town over by mostly businesses and the University.

Finally, I got to her building. And luckily she lived on the bottom floor. I knocked hard as hell. Knowing her and my sister wouldn't wake up if I didn't. Both of them were opposite of me and heavy sleepers like my daughter.

My sister came to the door and yelled through it, "Who is it!"

"Me!" I hollered back. She better recognize my voice.

She opened the door a crack at first, then seeing it really was me she opened it the rest of the way. Not wasting a second going off either.

"What the hell is going on? Are you kidding me? Why are you looking like that? What that nigga did now?"

She was wide awake now, her voice getting louder.

"Shhhhh. I don't want you to wake up mom."

"Too late. What is going on?" I heard my mother's voice come up from the dark hallway that led to her room and the back of the apartment.

"Nothing for you to worry about. I didn't mean to wake you up." I explained cutting my eyes at my loud ass sister.

My momma raised her eyebrows, came up, gave me a kiss on the cheek and patted my shoulder. Then placed another kiss on top of Amyra's head.

"I have to get up early for work. I love you. And you need to make sure to return my next phone call."

She turned around, tightened her robe and walked away. I didn't say anything back, thankful that she was tired and had to work in the morning. I didn't want to involve her in my mess if I could help it. She had enough to worry about with my two brothers and hardheaded sister. Which is another

27

reason I stayed away. My life seemed to be a constant mess.

I thought being with Khalil would bring more peace. But not now. Demont still was able to come after us at our own home. That shit wasn't safe. And the one thing Khalil definitely promised was that Demont wouldn't be a threat. He was wrong as hell about that one.

Right now I didn't have time to be thinking about him or any nigga for that matter. I needed to get away from here and put space between all this shit. Me and my daughter's safety was my number one priority from here on out. If Khalil couldn't be there when I needed him, it was still my job to protect myself and my child.

My sister walked into the kitchen and I followed, laying Amyra on the couch in the living room on the way.

"Really, what the hell is going on?"

"I don't have time to tell you details, but I do need your help. You know I wouldn't be here or ask if I didn't. Will you help me?" I wasn't telling her shit about tonight's events if I could help it.

"I'm gon' need something to go off. How you expect me to help you and I don't know what the fuck is going on? You show up here at 4 in the morning, with no clothes on like you been walking all night. I swear to God if that nigga laid his hands on you..."

"Me and Demont are not together."

"So it was another nigga?"

"No, no it's nothing like that. I promise I'll tell you everything later. But right now, I just need to get out of town and stay low key for a week or two. Until shit settles." I paused, putting my hands in front of me on the counter looking at my beautiful little sister.

Shonda was younger but bigger and thought she ran shit even though I was two years older than her. I loved my little sister to death but there was certain shit I wasn't telling her when it came to my personal life because she couldn't hold water. And then the next thing you would know my whole damn family and extended family would be involved in some shit that didn't have nothing to do with them. So the less she knew the better.

"Will you help me or not?"

"What do you need me to do?"

Less than an hour later we were back pulling in my momma's apartment complex and walking inside. I got out of Shonda's car and made my way inside right in front of my sister who had been driving my new whip. The one she didn't know I had until right before I told her what I wanted her to help me with. She didn't know anything. Not that me and Demont split, that I was in a new relationship or moved in a whole entire new house with a nigga my family never even met before.

She held her tongue, but from her demeanor I could tell she felt some type of way about just now finding out all of this. Especially like this. What could I say though? Hell, my own life had moved fast as hell these past couple of months. Maybe that was another red flag. That I needed to really back the fuck up and get my head on right. Which going away for a few weeks would take care of.

I didn't want to waste any more time staying here and making this shit hot for when Demont slept off whatever the hell he was on last night. And I really didn't want Khalil to come looking for me either. Even though I doubted he would. I mean the nigga didn't even answer my text. And when we went back he was nowhere to be found at the house. It was like he really didn't give a fuck about me or Amyra. So maybe everything was an act. It wasn't real enough for him to show up when it mattered anyway.

I said a quick goodbye to my sister, giving her a tight hug. Knowing she had my back and was down for whatever made me feel more like shit for staying away and keeping my distance. I silently vowed to change that when I came back. I was gonna make it a point of being closer to my whole family. After all, that was all you had for the most part.

I picked Amyra back up and took her outside. Placed her in the car seat and got my ass in the driver's seat. The sun was just coming up. Bright yellow, orange and pink rays of light shone across the morning sky. Such a beautiful fucking morning after a night of pure hell. I backed out and put the car in drive. Heading North and ready to get the fuck out of Wilmington. To forget this night ever happened. The nightmare was over. For now at least.

Khalil (King)

I drove up the block by my mothafuckin' self. My niggas were down the street around the corner. Pulled over, parked, and waiting on the side of the road. None of these North Side bitch niggas would expect for them to roll up. Not with me going inside the house solo. Which was the fucking point. All eyes would be on me. Niggas would be gunning for me, the way I wanted it. These mothafuckas thought they could come after us and that shit was gonna slide. They were pussy and stupid. Some coward ass shit was spraying bullets from a moving car. Standing eye to eye was some real G shit. But this nigga Desean was never official. He was always on that flaw shit. From day fucking one.

I pulled up on the block and parked my shit on the side of the street. Right in front of that nigga's house. The dumb mothafucka lived, ate, slept and shit at the same fucking spot he trapped out of. It was no secret how sloppy his team was with moving their weight. Which only showed how much of a rat he really was. He stayed out prison all this time. While making moves right out in the fucking open, you might as well say. Without a fucking worry since he was an informant. Ratting niggas out on both sides.

I stepped out of my whip. My new FN tucked in at my side. I didn't give a fuck how many niggas were aiming their tools at me, I was still walking inside strapped. We were about to see how this nigga played it. Since he talked all that big shit about being the fucking "boss" of the city.

Like I figured, these niggas stared and mugged hard as fuck but none of them said a single fucking word. I went in untouched and unfazed. What the fuck did I have to lose at this point? My nigga was in the fucking hospital and my bitch and daughter you might as well say was missing. I didn't fear any nigga walking before tonight as it was. And now I was out for blood.

I walked up to the door, where D'sean's right hand finally stepped in front of me before I knocked or opened the bitch. I ain't never had a problem with this nigga. Not before this shit. But that was all over with. I wanted all these mothafuckas dead now. Whether they were involved in the bullshit or not. Fuck them all and their fucking families.

"What's good nigga? You on the wrong side of town ain't you?"

"You know why the fuck I'm here. Move out of my way. Let your *boss* handle this."

I stared the mothafucka down. And caught the look on his face when I said his "boss" too. That shit stung his ego and it was written all over the nigga's face. He was salty as hell. On that jealous shit. I could read him like an open book. D'Sean's own fucking right hand wasn't on board and he probably had no fucking clue. That's the type of way these niggas moved. All grimy as fuck. Which is why it was only a matter of time before their whole operation crumbled.

He stepped aside though. And I opened the screen door. Walking inside the house. The front door already open, and I wasn't fucking knocking anyway. Stepping in their spot I looked to both my sides and didn't see any fucking body. The TV was on and curtains closed. It was dark as fuck. But when I looked straight ahead to the back of the house I saw the kitchen and a table. That nigga D'Sean was sitting at it with a stack of cash out. Counting it on the table with a bitch sitting on his lap rolling a blunt. All she had on was a bra and some panties.

This fraud ass nigga was sitting here like he was on some real kingpin shit when all he was proving to me was how fake he was. No real ass nigga sat with his door open and money out. He was way too fucking comfortable.

Seeing him made me want to pull my heat out and send a bullet between his fucking eyes. But I was playing it cool until I got my Imani back. She was my top priority and I needed to make sure she wasn't nowhere around this mothafucka before it was lights out around here.

"Look at this nigga walking in my fucking house. The fuck you want *King*?" All fucking cap like he ain't know why the fuck I was at his doorstep.

"I'm looking for Imani. You seen her?"

The only reason I stepped foot in this bitch was to make sure this nigga didn't have her here. I already knew he was behind Coup being shot and fighting for his fucking life. I didn't need verification and wasn't bringing the topic up. Fuck giving this nigga any sense of feeling like he won. This shit was against my pride as it was coming here to make sure Imani wasn't inside before lighting the bitch up. But I had to set that shit aside and not take the risk before calling the hit.

"Now this nigga can't keep his bitch in line." He looked to his right hand that was standing on the side of the table now.

Both of them laughed together about the shit he said. And I let them. Standing with my hands clasped in front of me, not finding a mothafucking thing funny but keeping a straight face. Biting my tongue.

"Like I said, You seen her or not? I don't know what your bitch ass brother got going on, but I'm coming to you. Straight up, seeing what's good. You got beef with me we can handle that shit. But when it comes to my family that shit's dead."

"Your family? Nigga, that bitch is bred and bought already. Look at my niece and know what the fuck you're talking about. How about you get the fuck out of here and if I see my brother, I'll let him know *his* bitch is back for the streets. But believe me her leaving your ass ain't got shit to do with us. That's on you my nigga. Now get the fuck out of here. You're lucky I ain't shoot your ass for this stupid ass shit. Next time you come back on this side make sure you got something worth fucking saying."

I nodded my head and walked out the same way I came. I wasn't here to go back and forth like a bitch. Like I said all I needed was to see his reaction when I brought Imani's name up to gauge whether he was telling the truth or not. He might have clowned me and even I could admit this was some weak ass shit to be doing. But at the end of the day I couldn't risk something happening to Imani behind my war with these pussy niggas. And I could show this nigga better than I could tell him. He might like to talk big shit but I was all action.

I walked out the front door and down the steps. About 6 niggas were standing around. A couple of bitches with them and a fiend here and there. All bets were off at this point though. These mothafuckas really thought they could come up against us and try and take Coup out without any kickback from us. They were about to be really fucking surprised.

I walked back to car and slid into the leather seat. Keeping one of the burner phones out on the seat, I sent a message with a fucking random ass letter to my lieutenant. And right after I pushed the button to start the ignition, I saw headlights from the SUV rounding the corner. Deja fucking vue, like a couple of hours ago with the mothafuckas gunning for us. It was the other way around now. I waited and pulled out right in front of the jeep. On fucking cue, bullets started flying. As shots fired from behind me. My window was already down and I was lighting these bitch ass niggas up along with my team. We stayed stopped in the middle of the narrow street, unloading our clips. And my niggas behind me came with extended bitches.

The niggas that were just on the porch were too slow or already ducked off inside. And that mothafucka D'Sean wasn't any type of fucking boss barely showing his face. Staying right inside the screen door without a gun in his hand. Just like a pussy ass nigga.

Sirens rang out in the distance getting closer every second. It was only a matter of time before they got here. We needed to hurry the fuck up. I laid my heat across my lap and looked over one more time. D'Sean was slumped over in the doorway, like he'd been hit by one of the bullets. I smiled and sped off. The jeep right behind me. Both sets of wheels screeched as we turned the corner and got the fuck out of this neighborhood. Away from these rats.

I damn sure wasn't going home either. We were headed up to Jacksonville to lay low and stay off the radar for the night. Already knowing this nigga D'Sean was a rat. So it was a fucking given he was gon' tell the law everything he fucking knew about our team. That was if he pulled through after catching a slug.

It'd be hard as hell to prove without shell casings to match the weapons though. Even with niggas talking. And these bitches would never be found. So the mothafuckas didn't have shit. We did shit so fast, without them expecting anything that all they could do was duck or run. And this was only the beginning. Like I said, it was war now.

Now all my focus went to finding Imani. She wasn't at D'Sean's spot and he wasn't in on it. All I could think was that nigga Demont had something to do with it. As much as I didn't want to lay this shit on Brandi with her already dealing with Coup in critical condition, I needed to see what she thought on the situation. It was time for me to figure out where Imani was and make sure she was brought home safe and fucking sound.

Imani

Rolling over, I instantly felt for Amyra. She was wrapped up in the blanket still sleeping peacefully. Thankfully she slept through most of the chaos last night and too young to understand the rest of the shit her crazy ass father pulled. As for me on the other hand, the events were still on repeat in my mind. I should have been able to get some good ass sleep once we got here. Instead all I saw was the evil ass look in Demont's eyes when he was high out of his mind pointing the gun in my face.

Dawn had come and gone. And I couldn't get more than a few minutes of sleep at a time. My body was sore as hell, but the worst hurt I had wasn't physical.

On top of the traumatic shit that I went through, I was fucked up behind Khalil. My supposed nigga didn't answer the phone, didn't come home, didn't protect us, and then wasn't even concerned enough to be home when I went back for my car. That shit hit me hard in the chest. Realizing the man you fell in love with and gave a part of yourself to, wasn't for you the way you thought. Not the way I was for him.

I knew one thing though, I wasn't a down and out type bitch. I'd never let a nigga break me down. I would simply do better in the future. Not get bitter, but get better. At least that's what I kept promising myself over and over throughout the night.

It was the day after Christmas and my life was in shambles. I was hiding out and needed to figure out my next move. Since I couldn't sleep, I sat up and stretched the best I could before getting out of the bed. Walked over to the window and pulled back the curtain enough to look out. It was a beautiful ass morning. That Carolina blue sky with no clouds even in winter.

Staring out in thought, I jumped from a knock at the door. My entire body on high alert. Still shook from last night. I hesitantly walked over to it. Fucking shaking. I was the furthest thing from a scary bitch. But last night had fucked my head up.

Looking through the peephole my entire mood switched up. Going straight to fight mode. Mad as hell to see the last mothafucka I expected to be outside the damn door.

King!

I stood still, not saying shit and not opening the door at first. I was stuck. But in a different way than the first time we reconnected. A few months ago I was in a trance like love at first sight. Now I was the most reluctant a bitch could be. This nigga did me dirty. He didn't answer and didn't show up when I needed him. And now it was a little too fucking late.

I didn't say shit, as I slowly opened the door. Ready to face his ass and get this over with. Keeping my palm open on the door's wood edge. Holding onto it so he couldn't get past. Ready to slam it in his face if needed. The sad part was, even now a part of me wanted him in the worst way. My mind said one thing, but my pussy seemed to have a mind of its own. That pissed me off more. I hated feeling out of control and betrayed by my own body.

Khalil stared deep in my eyes. Locking in with me.

"I'm sorry."

I shook my head no.

"I'm fucking sorry." He said again.

I just kept shaking my head back and forth. Quiet. My heart hurting. One tear fell. Then the rest started flowing freely after that. I dropped my hand from the door. Feeling the guard I had up against this man falling down too.

"I should've been there. I fucked up. I'm here now and I ain't goin' no fuckin' where shorty. I got you."

I turned around and walked with my back to him further into the hotel suite. My arms wrapped around myself. Wearing my black silk robe that I packed in my overnight bag. Then I sat down on the small pull out couch. But before I realized, Khalil was right there. Standing in front of me, looking down at me like only he could.

He reached out and grabbed me by the elbows. Bringing me right back up to my feet. Then lifted my body in the air. My legs automatically wrapped around his waist. Like all the other times. Our bodies knew each other well.

I let him kiss me deep and slow. Caught up in the heat of the moment. My instincts took over. I just needed to feel loved right now. Right or wrong it didn't matter.

Khalil carried me into the big ass bathroom and closed the door behind him. Sat me up on the marble sink countertop and then started sucking on my neck, gentle then rough. Biting and sucking turning me on more than I thought possible. He pulled open my robe and started sucking on my nipples giving attention to each one. Making them hard. My pussy was already leaking but my breathing picked up as Khalil's hands roamed rough as hell all over my body. Finding their way down to my thighs.

This nigga was in charge of every part of me and he knew that shit. With every touch and feel from his tongue my breathing picked up and I started opening my legs wider for him to get inside sooner.

He gapped my legs further apart with his big ass hands. Then he bent down, lifted my ass up off the counter and pulled my pussy up to his face. I swear to God when he took control there wasn't a damn thing I could do either. He had his way however he wanted me.

I leaned back, laying down so my back was flat against the cool marble. My robe some damn where, but not anywhere on my body anymore. Khalil began to suck on my pussy. That make up loving with his mouth first. He took his time and sucked, licked and flicked his tongue all over my clit. Not letting up. My hands found his head and held him closer while the rest of my body tried to fucking run from what he was doing to me. I'm talking about back all the way up to the damn mirror. But there was no space. Nowhere to move and he knew that shit.

"Stop running."

"I'm 'bout to cum!" I moaned. "I can't take it no more."

"Let that shit out. Don't fucking move."

I bit my bottom lip and watched intently trying not to move and keep still but my body moved in rhythm naturally with the flicks of Khalil's tongue. I rubbed my hands through his soft waves. But threw my head back the second he bit down on my clit. Sucking my damn soul out of my body. A big ass wave came over me and my knees and legs shook while his hands held them tight. Locking me in place like he wanted. Still, this nigga didn't let up. He sucked and slurped all of my cum. I couldn't even get out another moan, my breathing caught in my chest, from the pressure he was putting on my pussy.

I was exhausted by the time he was done and couldn't even sit up on the counter if I wanted to. Normally, I would've returned the favor and blessed him with some head. But I couldn't right now. Khalil must have realized how out of it I was from him eating my pussy alone. Because he sat me up himself.

And lifted me up. I wrapped my legs around him, and held on to his neck. With one of his hands he managed to lean in the shower and turn the shit on in between kissing me slow and sensual.

There were a lot of the times we fucked. I'm talking all out. Going hard. But the way he was handling me right now was different. I could tell he was fucked up behind what happened to me too. I didn't want his pity though. I just wanted him to be there for me when I needed him most.

I put that out of my mind and chose to let my feelings for this man take over. I loved his ass and as scary as that was, it was what it was. He had me. For better or worse. Until my heart said otherwise anyway.

Khalil walked us into the big ass stand up shower and let the glass door close behind him. Already steaming up. He took me over to the brown and beige slate wall and leaned me against it. My back against the cool tile, legs still wrapped around him and his hands gripping my ass. With the hot water falling on both of us.

I didn't give a fuck if my braids got wet at this point. All I wanted was to feel him inside me. My pussy was throbbing from what his mouth just did. Khalil continued kissing all over me, from my mouth, cheek to neck. He palmed my breasts roughly, pushing them up. Looked me dead in the eyes with me raised above him.

"I love the fuck outa you. You're mine. Ain't no running from this shit."

And with his last words, he slid his big ass dick in my pussy. All 10 inches all the way in. Going past my damn cervix straight into my stomach. I felt him everywhere.
It was complete pain and pleasure. He stayed still

waiting for my pussy to ease up and release the tight ass grip I had on his dick.

Continuing kissing me. Making my lips tingle from the electricity he sent through my entire body from head to toe. While filling me up with dick. Muffling the moan that came from his size.

I dug my manicured nails deep into his back, as he started moving in and out. Fucking me nice and slow, deep and hard. I had to move my hands up to his shoulders to try and keep him from going as deep as he wanted since there was no where to run with my back rubbing against the shower wall. Keeping my ass in place, this nigga picked up the pace.

Switching his grip from my ass to my thighs instead. And fucking me crazy.

"K-H-A-L-I-L! What the fuck!" I screamed.

This nigga was digging in my insides now.

"Take yo' dick shorty. You ain't leaving again are you?"

I shook my head no, biting my lip out of habit when this man was hitting my Gspot deep inside my pussy. He had me stuck. My body tensed up fast as hell with the waves of my climax getting ready to peak.

Khalil didn't like me quiet. Me not answering him or saying the shit he wanted to hear took him to another level. He got a look in his eyes. Like a true King ass nigga who got his way. His ass came in closer, leaving no space between us now. Our bodies pressed tight together. His dick all the way up in me. Then lowered my body down. My back and ass slid slowly down the marble wall. So that my feet were touching the shower floor now. Then he grabbed the side of my head roughly and turned my face towards him. Looking me right in the eyes again. Not that he wasn't looking at me before. But I'm talking that soul searching look. When our souls were connected from the way we stared at each other.

Then he let go, kissed my jaw, neck and shoulder. Turned me around. Slapped my ass. The sound extra loud from the water that ran down my back and the rest of my body. He knew I liked that shit. A little pain never hurt nobody. I turned around, looked over my shoulder and smiled at his ass. So he slapped my ass again this time harder. I gave an extra twerk in it for him. Arching my back. Knowing he wanted to fuck while watching my ass bounce back. Which was one of his favorite ways to have sex. And he could get it any way he wanted from me. He was daddy.

Khalil spread me wider and guided his dick back inside me. The minute he hit the base, I was cumming. Just that damn quick from the pressure he was applying. I leaned further down. And let my hands slide down the wall in front of me. Keeping my head down. I didn't feel any soreness in my body anymore. Only the feelings of ecstasy that my man caused.

He picked up the rhythm and started digging in my guts again. Hitting all of my spots. But not letting up this time. With deep strokes back to back. Holding me in place tight as hell on the hips.

I popped my pussy right back at him, on his big dick. Grinding back into him with every stroke.

"Just like that. Don't move."

Of course my hard headed ass didn't listen to shit my nigga said. I couldn't even if I wanted to. Not with the way he was fucking me.

"I can't take... it! Damn!"

"Yes, the fuck you can! Don't fucking move. What I tell yo' ass."

Khalil moved his hands up under me, cupping each of my breasts and pulling me into him. Forcing me to raise my head up and reach my hands up higher on the slippery wall. To brace myself. To an almost standing position. My body tingled all over. With the hot water making everything more slippery and wet. Along with my pussy dripping down all over the dick inside of me. Khalil let go of one of my breasts, and slapped my ass again hard as hell.

"Loosen up."

And on command, my body responded. This nigga could make me do anything without my brain being able to make sense of a damn thing. He kept his one hand on my ass cheek and squeezed it tight. Fucking me slow now, but somehow deeper. His other hand still playing with my nipple.

"Ahhhhh, I'm 'bout to cum again."

"Hold that shit."

"I can't." I whined.

Khalil stopped fucking me altogether. But kept his dick deep inside of me with his petty ass. Trying to make me do what the fuck he said. I already knew he didn't want me to cum again until he did. That way we could cum together.

I squeezed my pussy muscles on purpose around his dick. Gripping the hell out of it then releasing. Letting him feel it pulsing on his shit too. Two could play at that shit.

He pulled out, but kept the tip in and fucked me like that. Nice and slow but not going all the way in, making me go crazy. I lowered myself back down. Damn near touching my toes and the shower floor. Trying to back up the pussy on his ass. But he wasn't' going for it.

"PLEASE DADDY!" I begged.

And that shit did the trick.

"That's all you had to say bae."

He slid back in and went to work again. Picking up the pace and sending me right over the fucking edge. I started twerking on his dick the little bit I was able to. That made Khalil grab the top of both my ass cheeks and give me those final strokes I was ready for. His dick jumping at the same time my pussy convulsed again. I froze in place all of the sudden unable to fuck him back. My breath caught and not even aware anymore of the water showering down on our bodies. Completely full and feeling all the pleasure only this man could give me. I cummed all over his dick, making it rain in the damn shower. I felt his warm cum shoot out inside of me as he pulled me back into him in the last few fast strokes.

When he was finished, I was completely done for. Unable to really move that much. Khalil took the wash rag and lathered up soap on it for me. Taking his time to wash every part of my body. In a way that was so damn sensual and caring. I had never had a man attend to me the way he was. It was a different kind of intimacy.

And as exhausted as I was. Sore and ready to fall over. I found enough energy to return the gesture. I loved this man. I took my time rubbing down his broad shoulders, down the spine of his back. Kissing parts of his body like he did me. It was in the shower that I realized yet again that what me and him had was some different shit. It couldn't even be explained. I just knew that from this moment on things were going to be different somehow too.

Brandi

Day in day out, I stayed by Coup's bedside. I only left to go to class and that was it. I was so glad that this was my last semester and then I was done. I was worn down emotionally and physically. I knew I looked a mess and I even had lost 5 pounds and my ass was pregnant. Where does that shit happen? Where the scale goes in the opposite direction! I was looking rough too. But that shit didn't matter. I hardly slept. But that shit didn't matter. Coup is what mattered to me. He only had me, Lovely and King to look out for him.

That bitch that came by on day 1 didn't show her face again. She had some damn sense at least. At this point with how my nerves were worked, if she did attempt to show her face I was beating her ass on sight. I didn't give a fuck. I warned her ass, so that shit would be on her. And truth be told I could use a way to get out all the pent up emotions I felt out.

Yes, I loved this man. And carrying his child was a blessing that I'd come to accept. But at the same time I was up and down with how I felt on the daily. Some days I cared about being a mother and was optimistic like Coup was gonna pull through and shit would come together perfectly and then there were days like today where I doubted every single fucking thing. Doubted my ability to have a child. To love a man. And even if Coup would pull through or want a child with me.

I had started biting my nails. A bad habit I'd formed from the many hours spent up in the hospital room between studying and reading my ebooks on my phone. I looked out the window at the gray ass cloudy sky. Even outside was a mirror of how I was feeling today. Out of the corner of my eye, I thought I caught a movement from Coup's hand. But when I turned my head and stared hard at it. There was nothing. So I chopped it up to my mind playing tricks on me. It wasn't the first time. Sitting here made a bitch go crazy for real for real.

But then the monitors started beeping.

I stood up watching what was going on in front of me. Coup's chest was going up and down faster and faster like some shit was wrong.

"HELP!!!! HELP!!!" I screamed before grabbing the nurse's call button, regaining some control of myself for a second.

No shit like this had happened over the past month. My chest was going up and down just like Coup's damn near, in a panic. Two nurses and a doctor came rushing in. Talking and checking vitals. Walking on either side of the bed. I backed up and watched on intently.

"What's going on?" I asked.

But none of the mothafuckas working on Coup gave an answer. They ignored my ass, so I stepped closer to the foot of his bed watching.

"1-2-3" one of the nurses counted.

Then the other nurse pulled out the breathing tube in one motion as the doctor and other nurse helped to incline the bed and sit Coup

51

up. My man coughed a few times before his eyes slowly opened to small slits. The machines stopped the off the chain beeping, returning to a normal frequency. Shit all seemed good, but my brain wasn't connecting the damn dots. Was this all a dream, something I imagined? The answers to my silent questions came when I heard the voice I missed so much.

"Come 'ere." Coup's voice quieter than I'd ever heard it. But still the same deep baritone voice. Just with a scratchiness.

I did what I was told on the spot. The connection between the two of us making it like the nurses and doctor weren't in the room anymore. I walked up over to his side, and grabbed his hand. I noticed his wince when I did.

"Shit, I'm sorry bae."

"Fuck... all that." He sat up further a grimace coming across his pale ass features. Still, his light brown skin looked good as hell for being in the hospital laid up for a month.

I made sure to take good care of him, lining his shit up and everything. Giving him his sponge baths instead of letting the nosy ass nurses. Knowing they just wanted to touch what was mine. Yes, I was that kind of possessive. But Coup didn't need to know all that or how I had talked shit to each and every one of the bitches that I caught staring a little too hard. My man was fine, fine. And he still looked like a boss even in a coma.

"How's my baby?" I thought he was talking about me, until he reached out with his free hand that still had an IV in it and placed it on my stomach. Tears welled in my eyes. And I wasn't an emotional bitch at all. That shit was more like Imani than me. I mean she was strong as hell, but tears hardly ever fell from my eyes. Up until I was pregnant and in love with Coup's ass.

"Good." That was all I could say.

Nothing about me planning to get rid of the pregnancy needed to be mentioned. The fact was we were having a child together. Coup was going to come up out of this and all the shit I'd been praying for was happening. That's all that mattered. Shit was going to be okay. A heavy weight lifted off of me and I felt like I could breathe again for the first time since before Christmas night.

Imani

Now that I didn't have to work a part time job AND go to school full time chasing my degree, I was able to really focus all my attention on what I loved. And a bitch was thriving. I was turning out bomb ass food in my classes and the idea of actually owning my own shit one day wasn't so far fetched these days.

I had my own personal touch on my North Carolina BBQ recipe and was starting to add my choice of unique flavors to other dishes like my Mac and Cheese. Along with a few other secret touches on dishes that I was putting my foot in. The more thought and planning I put into the restaurant idea, the more support Khalil showed. This nigga was my number 1 fan and he was always saying the day I got that degree, he'd have another deed to put in my hands. A deed to my own damn restaurant. I blew that shit off. But here lately with the amount of money he was bringing in, it might be possible.

We weren't hurting before. But now shit was different. For the most part our day to day hadn't switched up much. It was the new security in place that was different. We had cameras damn near everywhere. Around the property and house. A new privacy fence was installed. No nosy neighbors or nosy ass people from different areas could see shit inside the fence. It made me feel safer and more secure. But at the same time the elevated security only meant one thing. Khalil was really that boss ass nigga now. Getting deeper into the game. And no woman in love with a man in the streets wanted that shit for one simple reason, his safety was at risk every time he stepped foot out of the door. I felt that shit to my core.

I brushed it off every day and kept my feelings to myself. I accepted this life so it was just no sense talking about it or stressing my nigga out. Especially when he had plenty on his plate. Hell, we both did for that matter.

I was walking out of my last class for the day, ready to go home and talk to my baby. That was another thing Khalil insisted that we get a nanny for Amyra. But that was where shit ended. I still cleaned and cooked. It was my house. And I got help from my nigga around the house. As much as he was gone handling his shit he still put forth effort every Sunday to help with chores and things. Making me feel like his queen.

There wasn't a damn thing I could complain about. I just hoped the next time I needed him he had my back the way he did all these other times. I wanted real. I wanted consistency. Matter of fact, I wanted it all!

On the way to my car I got a call from Brandi. When I looked at my phone I realized I had 2 missed calls. One from her and one from Khalil. I answered, hoping it wasn't bad news. My heart rate sped up, expecting the worst. That was the shit that went with loving a nigga in the streets. I held my breath after picking up and saying "hello".

"Sis, why you ain't pick up! I was going out my damn mind. Can you fucking believe it COUP IS AWAKE!"

"What?! Oh my God! Is he talking? Doing okay? What the doctors say?" I asked back to back questions. Excited as hell that my best friend would hopefully get some much needed rest and peace.

"Yes, yes, and yes! He's still got a ways to go and rehab. All that. But they say he's going to make a 100% recovery."

"Thank God! You want me to come by?"

"Nah, I'm good. I got somebody to talk to now. Well at least listen to my ass while I do all the talking. He can't really talk yet, but I won't complain!"

"I know that's right!"

"At least one of my damn friends gives a fuck. I swear to God... How 'bout when I called Takeya's ass she acted like she couldn't be bothered. Talkin' 'bout "so...." I had to check her ass real quick. Then she caught herself and tried to fix the shit. Switching up her tone. I don't know what the fuck her problem is, but I'm telling you right now if she comes with that bullshit to the party it's gon' be a problem."

Hearing Brandi tell me about Takeya should have been surprising, but it wasn't. Her ass had been going left for a minute. I just hoped she wasn't causing irreparable damage to our lifelong friendships. But one thing I knew, Brandi held a damn grudge. She never let shit go. Takeya was in the fucking weeds now. She better apologize or I

56

knew it would be a problem just like Brandi said. It wasn't the fact that she needed to like Coup or even care about his condition. It was about her supporting one of her best friends in a difficult time. If she couldn't do that, then she wasn't really for Brandi. And lately I doubted if she was in my corner either to be honest.

"What party?"

"The one ME and YOU are throwing, Duh. As soon as Coup is recovered we're going dumb. It's gon' be a movie sis!

"Aight, aight. You know I'm with the shit. You don't have to tell me twice! I'm here for it all!"

Our conversation put a genuine smile on my face. I hit the unlock button on my new car. Yes, a bitch was driving clean these days. A few months ago before I got with Khalil I had finally got enough coins together to buy my first real car of my own. It was used and had seen better days, but it was all mine. But as soon as we came back from out of town after Christmas, this nigga took my ass to the same place he bought his car and told me to pick out whatever one I wanted. I knew it was just another way for him to apologize and to try and fix shit between us, but no way was I turning down the offer. However he wanted to make things right, I'd let him. Including dick and gifts. I wasn't picky.

Naturally, I wanted to match my man. So I got a "cocaine white" as my King called it Hellcat to match his black one. We were like yin and yang to each other. The other half. All that corny shit. I was head over heels in love with this man.

When I was opening my car door and getting ready to set my books and purse on the passenger seat across from me a woman caught my eye. She looked so familiar standing on the corner of the sidewalk getting ready to cross the street to go to the other student parking lot. She had on a hat and a jogging suit that was all black. Nothing special. And I could only see her profile view. Still, there was the familiar look to her and I had a nagging feeling that I knew the woman. Whether from something good or bad, I couldn't remember. Instead of staring at the bitch like a weirdo, I went ahead and continued getting in my new car.

I always enjoyed the new car smell and comfortable leather interior. The inside was wood grain with the white leather seats keeping the theme from the outside going. Just sitting in the driver's seat each time put a smile on my face. All this nice shit didn't make me different but it did make me appreciate my circumstance more.

I went ahead and headed home, since Brandi told me not to stop by the hospital. It was still amazing that Coup was finally awake. I couldn't wait to see my nigga and put this pussy on him to celebrate.

I drove the 15 minutes across town and when I pulled into the driveway, Khalil's car pulled in right behind mine. That was the only thing missing from our house, a garage. But that shit was rare in the city even on a neighborhood residential block like the one we lived on.

I didn't even have time to step out of my car after leaning over to get my purse and books before this man made it a point to step to my door. Open it up and come in and scoop my ass up out the seat. Reaching down and lifting me up in a tight ass embrace. This was everything. His strong arms wrapped around me made me feel at peace and safe if nothing else did. Not to mention turning me on, it was on sight any and every time I laid eyes on my nigga. There was just something that only he did for me.

He didn't lift me all the way up this time, with my feet only a few inches off the ground for a split second. I could tell he was happy as hell to see me. And the butterflies in my stomach were there like always when I was in his presence. I swear this shit didn't make any sense. We both took our time kissing deep and slow enjoying each other.

He had been gone since Saturday morning and now it was Monday. "Handling business" according to his own words. I didn't know all of what that meant, but he was getting ready to tell me. He already let me know that things were changing. And told me that when he got back from his trip out of town, he wanted to sit down and talk about things. I had put that shit out of my mind, but now it came flooding back. I guess it was the intense look in his eyes. I knew some more shit was on his mind despite his excitement to see me. And happiness over his best friend coming out of a coma.

This nigga placed me down, slapped my ass and turned me around all at once it seemed. My head was spinning from the way his touch turned me on and how he handled me. Amyra was staying over at my momma's tonight with my sister watching her. The only good thing about the shit Demont tried to pull, was that I had gotten back closer with my family. Shit wasn't perfect but it was better. There wasn't that constant unspoken thought about how I should leave that nigga alone anymore. Because that was what the hell ended up happening anyway.

Khalil kept his arm wrapped around me, his hand pressed against my stomach and body close from behind while I led the way up the walkway and onto the front porch. His hold making me feel secure and turned on. The way he touched me never got old and always sent chills down my spine right to my pussy.

"Sit down beautiful." He slapped my ass as we came inside. Then closed the front door behind himself.

I went over to the living room couch and kicked off my Ones. Tucking my feet up under myself and rubbing them together like I always did.

Khalil walked into the room. My eyes watched his body and every move. He sat in the matching chair next to the couch. A few feet away from where I was leaned up against the arm of our couch.

"What is it? You got a look on your face that I ain't never seen before."

"I'm gon' be straight up. Bae right now we're swinging for the fences. I'm not even gonna front. It's gonna mean a lot more risk. But with Coup coming back, I know we gon' make it to the top. I just need you to hold yo' nigga down." He paused. Then continued talking. "Starting wit' you getting some protection for yo'self and Amyra. You can't be riding 'round without some heat. Ever! It's a lot of niggas gon' see me and mine as a target. I know you didn't sign up for this shit. And it's not forever. But it's right now."

"So what do I need to do? I know it's not forever. I believe you and I trust you. And for right now, whatever I can do to ease your mind I'll do. I see how hard you're going for our family."

"You mean that shit?"

I saw the vulnerability in his eyes when he asked. Staring back into his, I nodded.

"I got you too remember."

He nodded, bit his bottom lip and stood up. Came over to me and stared down at me like a hunter would his prey. I didn't mind though. That was what I wanted anyway.

Khalil reached down and grabbed ahold of my legs first pulling my feet out from up under me. Then he pulled me to the edge of the couch. Ass right up to the edge.

Kept that intense look in his eyes and watched me now like I did him when he walked his fine ass in to sit down. And I knew exactly what was coming next. I was getting some of MY dick.

I gazed back up at him, our eyes locked the entire time while he leaned down and pulled down my leggings that I wore to school.

Then he slid off my socks and kissed the soles of my feet lightly. This street nigga, King, who was solid and scary to the world was gentle as hell with how he was handling me. But I knew that wouldn't last. I smirked up at him.

"You gon' play all night or do somethin' for real." I winked, talking shit.

"Why you always wanna rush shorty. I got you."

And he wasn't lying.

Khalil (King)

A month came and went. I would say things were getting back to normal, but that was a fucking lie. On the home front me and the wifey were straight. She was opening her heart again and I was giving her time and shit. I couldn't fucking complain or expect her to be trusting of me when it came down to it and I wasn't there for her on Christmas night. I vowed to her and my fucking self that I would never let that happen again. It still fucked with me that I wasn't the nigga I told her I would be from day 1. And I was doing everything in my fucking power to fix that shit from ever happening again.

Security around our place was beefed up. Cameras covered the perimeter of the house and stayed on at all times. I couldn't let anything happen to the people I loved again. That shit was my first responsibility. Along with protecting came providing. Not one before the other. No more excuses. It was time to hold shit down like a real nigga was supposed to.

Coup was awake and out of the coma. My nigga had to relearn every fucking thing when it came to walking. But he was a natural born fighter. And that same killer instinct, look in his eyes, was coming back slowly but surely. It damn sure helped when I told him that the niggas responsible were already 6 feet under.

After the way shit went down, I stayed out of town for a week up in Jacksonville with Imani.

Then we came back. She had school and I needed to see what was good with my nigga and our business. It turned out there wasn't any real pressure coming at us behind the shoot-out.

That nigga D'Sean was one of the mothafuckas we laid down. He died on the spot. Right on his front porch after catching a bullet to the head. Two of the niggas on his team also lost their life. So as far as I was concerned shit was even.

That didn't mean I wasn't expecting and preparing for some pushback. Because those niggas had family members who would want some get back. That's just how war in the streets went. But what I did know was that we were the side with the bread and the resources to win. And if these North Side niggas knew what was good for them, they'd realize that shit before it was too late.

In the meantime I was all about fucking business. My dreams were unfolding in front of my fucking eyes. Once Coup was back in action, we were set. On the fucking come up like no mothafucka had seen around here.

Today I was heading out to Charlotte to meet Sergio at the new warehouse we were supposed to handle shipments out of. All of our product came through trucks. Straight up from Columbia, though part of Central America and then across the Southwest US. Before shipping out all over the damn country.

The partnership with Sergio and the Columbian Cartel had been building since the fucking beginning. The more shit we moved for him, the deeper entrenched I became in the cartel shit. That wasn't my goal but so far there'd been no problems. The nigga knew this wasn't long term for me. So as long as he remembered that, we were fucking good.

I was already on the way to the spot. Having been on the road a good hour. I'd be there by noon. Which was in time for the 1 o'clock meeting. I wasn't a nervous type of nigga. But I knew this meeting was a step up and shit was about to get real for us. I had to be ready. We decided to push back the club and concert promoting shit. Changing the plan for now. Instead we'd be opening up a string of arcades in Myrtle Beach South Carolina. An hour drive and out the fucking way of Wilmington. Keeping our main money washing operations off the fucking radar.

Including the weight that we could keep at them. We'd be taking a risk with cross state lines which meant trafficking charges would be on the table if we got caught up. But at this point dealing directly with the fucking cartel, every fucking charge was on the table if we got caught. So it didn't fucking matter. We might as well go all in. Up and down the coast.

Hopefully when all these fucking tourists went down there to spend money, the business would look legit since it was mostly cash coming in. The promoting shit wasn't hitting right now with concerts and shit being postponed. Being able to come up with new plans kept us ahead of the feds.

65

I put the business in my younger cousin's name. He was the only nigga in our crew without a record. And his ass was in college. He also had good ass credit from when his pops died and he got an inheritance off him being a veteran. Shit looked legit on paper. The nigga was trying to get his feet wet in the game, so keeping him out of the streets and on the business side was the best shit I could do for him and my auntie.

With the music bumping through my Hellcat's speakers, I zoned out deep in thought. Trying to make sure all bases were covered and there wasn't any lose ends. In the streets this shit was always life or death. Now more than ever. We had to make it. And the only way for me to get out one day was to go deeper into the bitch.

An hour later I pulled up to the address Sergio sent to the burner phone I had for the week. I changed out prepaid phones every week to keep the shit from being tapped. And I never talked to any mothafucka over the phone about a gotdamn thing. Too many stupid niggas forgot police could tap whatever the fuck they wanted. Giving up locations from data towers and whole fucking conversations. Niggas was even bold enough to talk on social media in DM's and shit. It was those types of niggas that would not be a part of our operation. Even on the lower level. Otherwise it was only a matter of time before we got caught up. And I wasn't going back if I could help the shit. I had too many other fucking plans.

The address in the GPS brought me to a Mexican store. It surprised me because Sergio wasn't fucking Mexican. He was Columbian and most of the time, shit was kept separate in the field for the two groups. I guess it was time to find out why the hell he called this meeting.

I messaged the nigga letting him know that I was at the spot early. Not expecting a response right away, but Sergio was on point. Sending me a message right fucking back. Instructing me to pull around behind the store.

At first I didn't see how. I kept looking and finally saw where he was talking about. Over on the other side of the building away from the neighboring strip mall stores. This place was separate and by itself, with an old white fence. Which was covered with overgrown plants. Creating privacy on all sides. Which was hard to come by in the city, but what was needed with moving weight.

I put my car in reverse, backed up and then drove to the side. Down the path, through the low grass that went around to the back of the building.

When I made it around the old brick building, the property opened up into a decent size dirt lot for what I assumed was loading and shit. There was also a shed a few hundred yards back before the tree line.

I was the type of nigga to take in every fucking detail. The next thing I knew, two Hispanic mothafuckas were approaching my ride. Both holding AK's with straps around their neck. Pointing their weapons at my windows as they walked up. I stayed straight faced and watched both them back. Sergio came out and stood by the back entrance to the store. Smoking a cigarette and talking to his right hand. The same man that was with him when we first set shit up at the restaurant in Wilmington.

I didn't pull my strap out, instead I kept it under the seat. This wasn't anything unexpected so I kept my cool and got out of my whip calm and confident. The type of nigga I naturally was. I didn't give a fuck about all that posturing bullshit. If today was my day to die, then so be it. A nigga like me couldn't fear a bullet.

Sergio raised his hand, "Es amigo bajen sus armas chicos."

I only knew a couple Spanish words. But caught the meaning from his tone and hand gesture. His goons lowered their guns and backed the fuck up. So shit was good. I understood this was all for show anyway. A show of power in the situation. I nodded my head towards Sergio.

"So, my friend are you ready to see why I had you meet me here?"

"I stay ready."

Sergio smiled and I knew this shit was about to be fucking big. He was in a good ass mood and only one thing could make a mothafucka happy like that. That was a fucking bag.

He walked back inside and I followed. The 2 men that approached my car stayed outside keeping watch. Inside the building there was more men standing around talking near a small table. A few were in a heated ass conversation, with cash in one of their hands. I didn't know what the fuck they were talking about, but I could tell the one nigga wanted to beat the fuck out of the other. All that loud ass shit talking stopped on spot when Sergio appeared. The same group of men stood up straight and got in fucking line. Literally lining the fuck up and waiting for instructions or to be acknowledged from their boss.

I watched the interactions paying close attention. Staying on my toes and taking notes for our own operation. Sergio waved them off and walked past, leading the way around the table. To the right side and through an entryway that had black thick plastic strips hanging instead of a door.

We were already in the back part of the good-sized Mexican store. So after going past the small doorway, moving the plastic back with my hand, we came into the storage area. Boxes lined the walls. Stacked on shelves with some on the floor.

The boxes were all different sizes and marked in Spanish writing so I didn't know what was inside. Sergio went over to one of the biggest ones closest to us on the floor. Then took out a sharp ass knife from the leather sheath in his belt. Like straight out of a fucking movie. This mothafucka was the picture of what you'd expect a cartel boss to be. I didn't have time to even soak that shit in. Here I was, a regular ass nigga out of Wilmington dealing with some big time shit. A lot had fucking changed and I had to be ready.

He cut the box open along the top. Opened it up and put his hand inside. Pulled out a bag of factory sealed empanadas and then cut into the bag. He held it up towards me.

"Look at this."

I leaned over and looked in the clear package. Then Shrugged.

"I don't see nothing."

"Exactly. Looks like fucking empanadas. Smells like fucking empanadas. But inside they're filled with pure cocaine. And the others..." He gestured with his free hand, still holding the knife, "More food. We got candy fucking paper diplomas. You name it we figured out a way to smuggle it in. All filled or covered in the product."

I nodded in understanding and a little amazement. This shit was fucking smart as hell. I knew the weight could be changed back into solid drug forms. I just wondered how the fuck they got all this shit past customs and immigration when it came across the border. And I wondered why the hell Sergio was bothering to tell me about it. There had to be a fucking reason for him to do that. And it wasn't because of fucking trust. Everything in this game came at a cost. Especially information.

"So why am I here?"

"You're a smart man, Mi amigo. I want to transport some of this to your new place of business. Of course... this will move you up from your current position. You'll be responsible for all of the distribution. From the moment the shipments arrive. I'll take care of the transports up until that

70

point. Do you think you and your team can handle this type of business?"

"Of course. I ain't never let you down before. I'll need to refigure a few things. As long as you remember I'm not staying in this shit forever."

"You might change your mind." He laughed still in a good mood.

"Nah, give me 2 years and I'm out. But my brother will be more than willing to take the reigns, you feel me."

"So we have a deal then." He reached his hand out for me to shake after putting his knife away.

"Damn right we got a mothafuckin' deal." I shook Sergio's hand looking him in the eyes.

Who the fuck would've thought my time away would turn out this fucking beneficial. That's how you knew shit was fucking destiny. Everything was coming full circle. I was ready as ever to be stacking some serious bread. I knew this meant different numbers though.

"So what are we talking 'bout exactly?" I asked as we walked out the way we came in. The men that were standing around the table on our way in were gone. The entire store was empty now. Quiet as hell.

"1/2 a kilo in every package give or take. White or brown. You'll get 5 packages a week to start. For your first location. That'll cut the price down to let's say 10 for brown and 12 for white."

"That works for me." There wasn't shit I could say against the numbers he was talking. This was the best deal a nigga could ever get. I'm talking a fucking dream deal.

"Now remember, no late payments, no fuck ups. We're good as long as you uphold your end. Entiendo?"

"Yes, we're good."

I left Charlotte after the meeting and hashing out the rest of the details. The first shipment would be coming in a month. That meant the business had to be up and running in South Carolina and I needed to change the way our operation handled shit in terms of positions.

We needed to turn the shit into a real business operation inside out and make sure there were no fucking leaks in our system. This was a time when I really needed my right hand fucking brother by my side. To talk shit over with and make the best decisions. That was how we had always worked and done shit to be successful. I didn't want to make any mistakes. So that was my next move. I hoped Coup was ready to jump back in full force because we were better together.

Coup

Waking up to a fucking bullet hole in your chest will have you reevaluating a lot of shit. First thing was my down ass bitch who hadn't left a nigga's side. I knew her ass was pregnant before I got temporarily taken out. I saw a message left by the clinic about her appointment. You gotdamn right I looked up the address, and it showed up a fucking planned parenthood.

I was out of it in a damn coma but not dead. I couldn't remember shit, but it seemed like the past few however many days, I'd started hearing voices and shit around me in what seemed like a dream. I heard Brandi cussing at the nurses and then turn around and say a prayer over a nigga. If you ever had your woman pray over you that spoke to your soul. I knew she had better not gone through with no dumb shit and got rid of my seed.

Lucky for her ass, when I did wake up and ask about my baby, touched her stomach, she gave the right fucking answer. I didn't know if we could make it if she had done some stupid shit like that. Even an unplanned seed was a gift. No way was I gonna go out like a sucka ass nigga behind mine.

Today was my release day from this bitch. I was going the fuck home. With physical therapy every day for the next month. The doctors said I would make a full recovery. I was going for shorter than that. I knew my nigga needed me back in the streets with him. He had been holding shit down and I expected nothing less. The same I did when

73

he got locked up. But together we were fucking unstoppable.

Starting with making sure those pussy ass niggas from the North Side were out of the fucking way for good. Since we were in the hospital and couldn't be sure of who was listening and what not, King was keeping shit under wraps. As soon as I was out this bitch, we were going to clear everything up whether I was still recovering or not.

I already hit King up and let him know what time to stop through my spot. Brandi took off another day of school to drive me home. I told her she didn't need to be doing that shit. Putting her future in jeopardy. But her hard-headed ass wouldn't take "no" for an answer.

How could I complain when she walked in looking like the finest bitch a nigga ever laid eyes on. When I say mine was the baddest, I meant that. To me she was the whole fucking package.

She was wearing some cut out jean shit showing off a lot of fucking thigh and a crop top with a zip up hoodie. If she didn't have that shit on, I would have made her go put some other shit on. What was mine was mine. Some niggas liked to flaunt their bitch, and that wasn't even what I was against. I just wasn't up to murdering some disrespectful niggas on my way out of the hospital. Ol' girl had to cut that shit out for a minute. She was always wearing little ass shit.

As drained as I was feeling, I wasn't showing a fucking weakness to not one of these nurses who might go run and tell it to their nigga. Who might be a fucking enemy. Call me paranoid, but it's just what the fuck it was at this point. At least until I got some answers this afternoon.

Brandi came up, trying to get behind the wheelchair that I was in. Ready to push me out. Without saying shit. I could walk, but it was the only way to be discharged. Plus I didn't mind letting my bitch cater to me. What wasn't happening was her ignoring her nigga. She wasn't used to me being back up and about yet. Because she would've known what that would get her ass. As much as it hurt to move my right arm with the chest wound still not 100% healed, I reached out and gripped her forearm stopping her from walking all the way past.

She looked down, surprised. Eyebrows raised.

"You know better than that."

"What?"

I stared at her hard as hell. "That's how you greet yo' nigga. I can see I been out of it too long, yo' ass forget how shit go." I rubbed my fingers over her warm skin.

And noticed the way her muscles tensed up from her arm to her frown she was wearing with those pouting ass lips. Looking real annoyed with my ass just the way she always did when she wanted some dick.

But her ass leaned down and gave me a deep ass kiss. That same spark was there like it never fucking left between us.

75

"That better daddy?" She stood up and adjusted her shirt and pants like we were really doing something. Still with attitude that only she could pull with me.

I slapped her fat ass and nodded my head. Letting her get behind the chair and get me the fuck out of this place. I was ready to get home, and get some pussy. But it was business first then I was tearing that ass up.

Usually we would have met up at our Central house to go over business. But with me in this condition at least for a few more weeks it was just easier to talk shit over at my place. It was only me and King. Our women were in the kitchen. It was a type of coming home get together with the 4 of us. Imani was throwing down in the kitchen and luckily my appetite was somewhat back because she could fucking cook.

"Let's get to it. Fill me in on everything I missed nigga."

"We went back and laid them niggas down like I said. It was lights out for D'Sean the minute he sent the hit on you. He should've known better. But since he didn't him and his team is fucking history."

"But not all them mothafuckas gone."

"Nah, it's a few left. Word is they're trying to reach out and make amends. I haven't fucked with the idea to be honest. It don't sit right with me. But now that you're home it's some bigger shit we got on the table now. I'm talking truck loads coming in. I went out to Charlotte and Sergio brought me to the fucking store where the product ships to. We gon' have to expand further to push this type of weight bruh."

"Who you say is left on the other side?"

"Rico, you know D'Sean's right hand. Big mothafucka."

"I know who you talkin' 'bout." I nodded my head. "Who else?"

"It's a few low level niggas. Nobody to worry about. Corner boys and shit. Otherwise the only nigga really left that shouldn't be breathing is hiding out somewhere. Fucking Demont. And it's some more shit... So that night you wasn't the only target. This nigga go and walk up on my fucking front porch, ring my doorbell and took Imani and Amyra. Holding them at gunpoint and shit. She says he was on that shit. But I don't give a fuck. The fact he was able to comfortably come up in my fucking yard and then touch MY family fucks with me. What kind of nigga can't protect his family and is in the streets? I got niggas trying to locate him as we speak. I'm just waiting for his bitch ass to turn up. He's too stupid to last much longer on the run. Then it's lights out. The nigga's days are numbered."

"Damn nigga. As soon as he's out the way, you know what we gotta do though."

King nodded, already knowing what I was thinking he said, "Bring the city together."

"Exactly. We can't be at war and winning at the same time on our home turf. We need shit smooth here so we can move on other territory. Because with the kind of weight you're talkin' 'bout we gon' have to step on some other nigga's toes. You feel me?"

"Yeah, but we gotta take out this nigga first."

"Already." I agreed with King. It was the principle of it all and the fact that this nigga was still breathing made us look weak. More than that, I knew that bullshit was eating my nigga up.

King offered me the blunt he was smoking, but I turned the shit down. I didn't want to fuck up my progress with physical therapy in any way. I needed to be back working like yesterday.

"The food is done ya'll!" Brandi yelled out to us standing by the sliding door to the back porch where we were.

King opened the door first and I followed taking my time coming in. When I came in Brandi was waiting right where she had called us in from.

"You good daddy?" She checked on me.

I reached over and slid both hands around her body. Grabbed her ass and pulled her into me. She seemed surprised as a mothafucka. From my actions being I was still recovering and because I know she felt my dick against her stomach.

She looked up, eyes intense as fuck. Just the look alone telling me what I already knew. She was ready and wet for her nigga already.

I placed a kiss on her forehead and then let her go. And kept walking into the kitchen to fix my plate.

I wanted her to take care of me don't get me wrong. But she also needed to remember who her nigga was and I was still in charge. In all ways.

King

We were dong it big this weekend celebrating a whole lot of big shit we were in the midst of. First Coup was back on my side again. 3 weeks out and he was back like he never fucking left. Holding shit down and bringing that leadership that he naturally had with this street shit. Always hands on and the one to do the talking. Keeping all the niggas on our team in line.

Our new skate rink with arcade was opening up on Monday, with the finishing touches happening this morning. Which is why I was down in South Carolina at 8 am instead of enjoying some pussy like I usually did before I got ready for the day and left. Taking care of business was a priority, so I was here at 5 am with the contractors. All I was waiting on now was the last permits to come through.

It was a good fucking day and I had a surprise for Imani tonight that I knew she was gonna be excited about. She had really held a nigga down since the day we met, but especially after that shit at Christmas. When the world made you feel like you were less than a man you were lucky if you had a real woman in your corner to speak to the King in you. Imani could've walked away when I couldn't protect her or Amyra, but she chose to stay and trust me to get shit right in the future. That shit meant the world to me and there was no way I was letting her down. I was determined to live up the man she saw in me.

My mood got fucked up the minute I saw my ex's number flash across my cell. After Christmas night, I'd been keeping Rosaria's bank account filled with direct deposits weekly. That way she had no fucking reason to hit me up. I read up on her being able to get an early paternity test with some new shit they had. But I had held off on that even because I still hadn't told Imani.

I planned to keep it real with her the same fucking night. But the way everything went, I looked at it like there was bigger issues to deal with at hand.

All her calling now did was remind me that I was sitting here on the same type of shit Imani's ex was on and the way he did to her. Not that was trying to be. But that was how Imani would look at it. Especially the longer I waited to tell her. Fuck it, I was telling her tonight before the party. It didn't even fucking matter. I couldn't have her find out from the streets and bitches talked. She'd hear the shit straight from my mouth.

I reluctantly answered. Fuck it. Better to get this shit over with too.

"Hello!? King!?" Rosaria's voice started off with fucking attitude.

I shook my head, "What's good? Why you hitting my line?"

"You know why I'm calling nigga. It's time you step up in a more personal way. I don't know why you act like I'm a stranger or somethin'. Before your new bitch, I was the only bitch."

"Aye, don't come at me talkin' bout my woman being disrespectful. Get to the fucking point Rosaria. What do you want?"

"Like I said, I'm showing now going on 6 months. I want you to go to the doctor's appointments, start building a bond with *your* son."

"You having a boy?"

"Yes, *your* son! And I'm making him a Jr."

"Whoa, whoa you need to slow down. I don't even know if the jit's mine yet. I'm gon' come wit' you though. We need to get a test anyway."

"Nigga, I know who my baby daddy is! But you want to act stupid, fine! The appointment is next Thursday at 2. I'll send you the address."

"Aight."

Rosaria hung up on my ass and I was glad. Shit, she could be mad and all in her feelings all she wanted. The truth was she was out here fucking around instead of holding me down while I was locked up. It was no telling who the baby's father really was and I wasn't going out like a sucka. Fuck that.

I rubbed my hand over my forehead, putting my phone back in my pocket. I knew until I told Imani about this shit, my day was fucked up. She might leave my ass for real but the shit was before her. So she was gonna have to understand or if the baby was mine, she was better off leaving if she couldn't accept him into our family. I would never turn my back on my seed. If it was mine that is.

An hour later, I was heading out after signing all the paperwork for the licenses. Ready to see

Imani. The 2 hour ride gave me time to get my head together. All I could do at this point was keep it real.

When I walked in, it was to some good ass smelling food cooking. My stomach started fucking talking. I hadn't even realized I was hungry. Imani was the truth and kept a nigga fed. She really loved this shit.

When I came in, I saw her greedy ass sitting down at the table eating a philly cheesesteak and some homemade fries. A salad on the side. When she cooked she did everything with extras. I wasn't complaining. Amyra was in the living room watching some gaming shit on the TV the kids played.

Leaning down, I kissed the top of Amyra's head and went into the kitchen looking to fix my plate first.

"I already fixed your plate bae. It's in the microwave."

"I love yo' ass."

"You better not just love me because I can cook either."

"You know better than that, it's the pussy too." I joked.

"Mmmmhhhmmm."

She went back to eating after laughing. I got my plate and sat down with her after pouring a glass of lemonade.

I started eating and looked up after half was gone.

"What is it?"

"What you mean?"

"I can tell when something's on your mind. You get this look in your eyes. Where you here, but you not really here. Like you in a daze."

Damn, she knew my ass too well.

"I got something I need to tell you."

"What is it? Just say it." She gave her full attention to me. Partly turning in her chair to look right in my eyes.

"When I first got out I fucked my ex one time. It was before you. Now she saying she pregnant and it's mine."

Imani sat still and quiet for a few minutes. I waited. Then reached out for her hand.

"Do you think the baby's yours?"

"Might be. I can't say it ain't for sho'. But this don't change nothing between us or our family .What we got."

"Oh, it changes EVERYTHING if that's your child. I shouldn't feel some type of way because it was before me. But I don't like the shit. It is what it is. I'm just glad you told me so I didn't have to find out from somebody running their mouth. No wonder why that bitch was acting funny when she saw me."

"When did you see Rosaria? You ain't say nothing to me 'bout it."

"Why you worried then?" Imani turned her head to the side ready to talk shit.

I was smart enough to shut the fuck up. When your woman gave that look, it meant to drop it. At least the weight was lifted off my shoulders from the shit.

Now I wanted some of MY pussy. I was a needy ass nigga when it came to Imani. And no other bitch was doing it for me besides her. Niggas was either faithful or not. And I was one of them when it came to a loyal ass woman. She was the only one for me.

I stood up from the table, took both our plates into the kitchen. Imani went to do the dishes in the sink, but I grabbed ahold of her arm and pulled it up to my lips. Laid juicy ass kisses on her forearms up to her elbow. And like I knew, her body was ready for me.

I walked her pretty ass down the hall and right the fuck into our bedroom. While Amyra was occupied, it was time to taste and play in her sweet ass pussy before we got ready for the party tonight.

"Baby, I'm ready!"

"Damn, that's what I'm talkin' 'bout."

I couldn't help but lick my lips watching Imani walk towards me. I put my glass of Dusse down after throwing back the last of the drink I was sipping on. Getting my mind right. Ready to enjoy this fucking night.

My nigga was back and we were on top. The whole fucking East Side was winning right now on the street shit and the legal grind. I lit up the Kush that I rolled into a blunt. Keeping my eyes locked on my woman. She was wearing some little ass shit.

But I didn't mind. She was in good hands tonight. I wasn't her last nigga. I would show off her sexy ass any chance I got. Only insecure niggas tried to downgrade their woman. And she was matching my fly perfectly tonight. Both decked out in denim and black.

Imani came up beside me. I pulled her into my side with my free hand. She was on her bullshit tonight though and cozied herself right up in front of me. Ass pressed into me with her small dress coming up higher on her thighs. She reached behind herself, moving to the side just enough. Smiled and took the blunt. Imani wasn't a smoker but when we were turning up she liked to get a few pulls from the blunt.

We headed out and I was feeling like the fucking King with his queen right by his side, where she should be. Walking into the club all eyes were on us. Mothafuckas damn near parted ways while we walked over to the VIP section to join the rest of our crew.

I dapped up Coup who was sitting comfortably on one of the lounge chairs. It was good music and nothing but good ass vibes. Right away the ladies linked up, standing up like it was their spot. Over by the edge of our section that overlooked the main floor. It was dark, but the light was shining on them and they didn't disappoint.

Imani and Brandi were singing along to the lyrics of the song the DJ was playing while me and Coup watched. We were deep as a mothafucka in here. Niggas better not come on that bullshit tonight.

About an hour after we showed up, I had to do a double take looking over by the bar. To the same damn place I had spotted Imani the first night I ran back into her. Shit was like déjà vu, but this time it was the opposite effect. My eyes weren't playing tricks on me, because Coup tapped my shoulder and nodded looking at Rosaria like I was. This bitch was standing by the bar in some little ass dress and a round full stomach. Out on a weekend in the middle of the night. It was already around 3 in the morning. And here this bitch was acting like her ass wasn't pregnant. And with my seed according to her.

I started walking off in her direction, to send her ass home. I don't know who the fuck she thought I was. But she must have forgot the type of nigga I was or she'd known better. By the time I made it to her, there was a space cleared like niggas knew I was on my way and they better stay the fuck back.

"Yo, what the fuck you doing here? You pregnant and out like a hoe. You need to take yo' ass home now!' I grabbed Rosaria by the elbow and started taking her ass out the fucking front of the club.

"Get the fuck off me king! It's none of your concern where I'm at or what I'm doing. Nigga, the only thing you need to worry about it that bitch you came with. NOT ME or MINE! Believe that."

She turned and pointed that sharp ass nail right in my eye. Getting the shit close as hell.

I didn't say shit else. I squeezed her arm harder and pushed her in front of me. Making her feet scoot along the gotdamn floor. I didn't give a fuck about all that shit she was talking. I had the mind to slap her in the fucking face for how stupid she sounded right now. But I wasn't getting into it with shorty. She wasn't mine. But the seed she was carrying might be. And for that, I would make sure certain things was done right.

I got her outside, and told her ass to go home one more time. She looked at me like she was ready to curse my ass out but she turned back around and walked down the sidewalk towards the parking lot. I waited and watched until she was at her car. Which was nicer than the shit she left my spot in. I took a mental note of that shit. She was pushing a new black Benz.

The minute she was in the car I got my ass back inside and walked through the crowd again. Up over to the VIP section. Looking around I saw my team and Coup with the rest of the bitches and niggas from the East side. Any and everyone that associated with us was having a good ass time. Brandi was close up on Coup. But Imani was nowhere in sight.

Imani

Man this shit was not how I wanted the night to go. I guess I should be thankful King told me about his ex being pregnant before seeing the shit first hand and being caught off guard. But the shit that was the last straw wasn't the hoe being pregnant. It was the fact that my nigga tended to her like she was his.

That was it for me. I already went through this bullshit with Demont. I wasn't about to go through none of it again. These niggas wanted to fuck and not use protection, then they had to deal with the consequences. That didn't mean I had to. I might be a down ass bitch, but I could choose what and how much I dealt with.

And the disrespect was a fucking no-go. My man should never take off after another bitch. EVER!

"Come on let's go to the bathroom."

Brandi reached out locking her arm in mine. I walked out of the section and over to the bathroom. Opposite from where King was having his little scene go down.

"I gotta get out of here. Right now! I'm not doing this shit."

"Whatever you need sis. I'm with you. King's foul as hell for that shit and he know it."

"Nah, I don't think he does though. It don't matter. I been here and I'm not doing this shit again. It is what it is. He fucked up. He'll find out when he realizes I'm gone. But he might not even notice." I shrugged.

Brandi gave me a light hug. Rubbed her stomach. "Okay, let's go." She added.

"No, I'm not dragging you into this. It's a celebration for your man tonight. Stay, enjoy each other. Don't let our fucked up relationship get in the way of yours."

"You sure?" She questioned. "You know it's no questions asked when it comes to you. No matter what I got going on."

"I know and I appreciate it. Let me slide out. If you can just don't say anything to King and let me drive your car home. That's all I need. I'm good."

"Alright. Let me walk you out the back then. Make sure you're straight at least. I'll wait and then tell Coup so he can figure out how we're getting home. He's gon' be pissed, but I'll make it up to him at home. Put this pussy on him and suck his dick real good. "

"Ewwww, bitch. I know your nasty ass will too."

Brandi laughed and I nodded. We walked out of the bathroom and found the side exit down the hall. I pushed the door open and felt the cool breeze hit my cheeks first. Brandi stayed true to her word and waited and watched. Holding the door open.

Around the corner, I spotted King's ass standing by the front entrance watching Rosaria get into her car. I paused and stopped right in my tracks. Waiting. Until he was done being the "good" nigga he was, seeing her home and shit. The minute he turned to go back inside, I slid my body closer to the building and out of sight from him. Then waited about a minute and stepped back out past where the bouncers were standing near the entrance. Luckily King was back inside. So I hurried the fuck up. Damn near running to Brandi's new car that Coup bought her. Like always I was thankful as hell to have a real ride or die friend.

As soon as I was home, I went ahead and got comfortable. Undressing completely inside the bedroom. Then I got under the thick down blanket and wrapped myself up in it. At least it could give me some comfort because I was done putting up a strong front.

When my head hit the pillow, the tears started coming. Seeing that shit tonight hurt. I cried silently. Then my phone started buzzing next to my head where I laid it. I saw that it was King and sent his ass right to voicemail. Ignoring him. All I wanted to do was go to sleep and forget about that bitch and him.

But then the phone started buzzing again back to back. Fuck that! This nigga had caused me enough hurt tonight, I didn't want to hear shit he had to say. I powered the phone off. Fuck King and fuck his fucked up ways. I was tired of being let down by him, when he promised to do the opposite.

I drifted off to sleep with a blank mind. It was already made up. I was just gonna leave King's ass alone for good and not speak to his ass if he came home. I was done with the disrespect and bullshit.

Next thing I knew, I felt the big ass comforter being pulled off my body and was immediately pissed off. Being woke up to more bullshit! Khalil was standing by the foot of our bed. Glaring down at me with the bright ass light turned on and shining in my eyes. The look on his face told me he was ready to battle. But that was okay. He could get some back too if that's the type of shit he was on. I went to sleep in my feelings and being woke up like this only added fuel to the flames.

"What the fuck KING! I was asleep…"

"You really on yo' bullshit tonight. How you gon' leave yo' nigga in the middle of the fucking club without saying shit. You wrong as hell for that shit shorty."

This was the first time Khalil ever talked shit to me. Raised his voice or showed anger. But I didn't give a fuck. GOOD! It was about time he get a taste of his own medicine. I was loyal to a fault and he didn't give me the same back. It was like I was thinking earlier when I fell asleep. Fuck King! And I meant that shit.

"Nigga, you wrong as hell for entertaining yo' ex. Right in my face and for the whole damn city to see. Miss me with the bullshit KING! I guess we're even now. Matter of fact, we're NOT even. I don't even want to talk to your black ass right now. Go sleep on the couch or wherever that bitch at. Go find her. I don't give a fuck no more."

Khalil walked over to the side of the bed. Coming closer to where I was laying. Leaned down low to get in my face. Looking straight into my eyes.

"That's what you really want?" He asked.

I paused, and stared back. "Yes." I answered.

He nodded his head, stood all the way back up and walked out of the room. A lump in my throat formed, but I held that shit in and closed my eyes. I waited and held in everything. Up until the bright ass light irritated my nerves so damn bad. And the coldness from the room penetrated my bones, causing me to get up. Knowing that Khalil was gone, having left the house. Even without hearing the front door open or close or his car's engine turn on. I knew he was gone.

I walked over to the edge of the bed, picked up my big ass comforter, then turned off the light. Got my ass back in bed and laid there numb to it all. My heart and mind at odds with each other. I couldn't cry or nothing. I just laid still and took in as much warmth as I could from the blanket and darkness.

Coup

Looking at the screen and seeing my seed was the best feeling in the fucking world. When the doctor wrote out at the top of the picture *"It's a girl!"* I knew shit was changing for a nigga. I respected women for the most part as long as they respected themselves. But knowing I'd be responsible for raising, protecting and making sure my own seed was good in this world was a different type of thinking. That hit me right when I saw the shit.

Brandi's fine ass was looking up at me crying. I swear she better be crying some happy tears because otherwise I was gon' want to go upside her head. My bitch was thorough as hell but this being a mother shit was still fucking with her. She needed to get her shit together before our shorty was here. I had been supportive and understanding but at some point Brandi had to step the fuck up and get out of her feelings. She thought she didn't have it in her to be a mother and shit. It was the stupidest bullshit I ever heard.

"Why are you looking at me like that?" She waited until the doctor stepped out to ask. While she stood up and pulled her leggings up.

I stood up from the chair and came up close to her. Placed my hands on her small but rounded stomach.

"I'm a lucky ass nigga. What can I say? This right here is my everything. You understand?" I went up under her tight T-shirt and felt the bare skin of her stomach.

"I know. I just wish..."

I took my other hand and put my finger over her lips to stop some stupid shit from coming out of her mouth. I knew Brandi better than she realized. Which is how I found out she was lying to a nigga and pregnant in the first place. She was about to piss me off. And I was in a good ass mood, feeling on top of the world. Here I was just having come out of a coma back from the fucking dead, with the woman of my dreams who had my fucking heart. And now a daughter on the way.

But still all Brandi saw was the bad shit. The doubts and insecure shit was pissing me off. It was selfish as fuck. Especially right now. I wasn't going for it.

Brandi saw my mood change too and her ass shut the fuck up. Which was in her best interest. I was still happy as fuck to find out I was having a daughter. But it was no denying Brandi fucked up my mood still. As much as I didn't even let her say shit.

I didn't even wait for the doctor to come back in and give Brandi her papers and shit. I turned the fuck around and walked out of the room. Left out the building and went and got the car. Pulled up to the entrance in the parking lot and waited for Brandi to walk out with the car running.

She came out about 15 minutes later. Walking slow as hell. Acting pissed off. She slammed my door when she got in too. I knew she was trying to get a rise out of me but I wasn't going there with her. I didn't say shit. Turning up the music in my old school and driving to our house. When I pulled into the driveway, I put my car in park but kept it running.

Normally we would have had a whole fucking conversation on the way back. But it was silent as fuck between us.

"Really Coup? You ain't got shit to say to me? Why are you acting like this?"

"I'm 'bout to head out and check on some things."

"Are you fucking serious right now?"

"Nah baby are YOU fucking serious? You need to step the fuck up and stop bullshitting. You 'bout to be a mother and you crying like it's the worst thing in the fucking world that's happening to you. You act like carrying my daughter is ruining your life. All you thinking about is yourself right now. And I ain't going for it. Shit's weak as hell. I didn't take you for that type of woman." I shrugged. "Like I said, I got some shit to handle. I'll be back later."

"Don't even fucking bother! Fuck you." Brandi said.

Getting up out of the car, speaking calmly back to me. Not yelling but sounding defeated instead. Tears really coming down her face now.

But like I told her I wasn't going for the weak shit no more when it came to her being a mother. I couldn't accept the shit. Not when it came to my daughter's well being. She needed a mother who wanted her. Not one that doubted and didn't want her.

Brandi tossed the sonogram picture at me before slamming my door again. Yeah, that shit pissed me off with the fucking door and how much I loved my car. Brandi knew that. But right now I didn't even give a fuck about that either.

I waited until she was in the house to pull off. Then backed out of the driveway. Heading to the one place I knew I could release some of my frustration. I knew I was wrong for this shit, but right now I really didn't know if me and Brandi were going to make it. Maybe it was for the best if we stay apart. That way she could figure out what the fuck was really important. Because in my opinion her number one priority should be our child. End of story.

Imani

March was just another reminder of the one thing I was trying my hardest to forget. The nigga who considered him "King" around here. At least with school and my busy ass schedule, the last few weeks had gone by fast as hell. Even if I did cry myself to sleep most nights. Missing the same man that I wanted nothing to do with. Like they say there's a thin line between love and hate. So instead, I chose to keep my eyes on graduation and the future. Reminding myself over and over that I couldn't control anyone but myself. My own actions and decisions. King had a new family and that's just how shit went.

I had my own daughter, own ex and own shit to deal with. Including the fact that I was out here on my own now. I owed it to myself and Amyra to hold shit down to the fullest and be the best mother and woman I could be. Fuck a nigga and fuck King. The shit hurt, but I'd get over it. The same way I did everything else that was meant to destroy my peace. Life went the fuck on.

"Mommy. Book please." Amyra held out the new book I brought home for her.

I pulled her small body onto my lap, up on the couch. Sitting cross legged while opening it up and then read it nice and slow. Taking my time. Enjoying our time together. With how busy I was, I still wanted my daughter to feel how important she was to me. She'd already had 2 father figures

98

uprooted from her life. I vowed to not let that shit happen again.

It's been almost a full month since I'd seen or heard from King but everything reminded me of him. So much so that I had to box up all his clothes and shit. I set it all in the walk in closet and got all my things out of there. Then closed the damn door.

If he wanted any of it, he could come get it when I wasn't around. But other than that I had made it a point of mentally and physically trying to move the fuck on. Cooking was like therapy for me. Without that I knew I would have sulked and sat here feeling sorry for myself.

I didn't have classes today and it was Friday which was the one day out of the week I took for myself. Shopping, relaxing, and pampering myself. Whatever I could get away with. The account Khalil set up for me was still stacked with money. I was done with his ass but not above spending the money. What we had might be over but I was far from dumb. I wasn't trying to run through it though so I only spent what I needed with the occasional treat for myself. Money never did shit for me, but I'd be lying if saying life with King wasn't easier when it came to not worrying or wanting for shit.

I dropped Amyra off later than usual to daycare. I let our nanny go a few weeks ago. It just didn't feel right anymore. Then I headed to my waxing appointment. An hour after that, I went and got my eyebrows threaded and tinted. My next stop being the mall.

When I tried to call Brandi to see if she was free to meet me, she sent me to voicemail and didn't answer my text. I was gonna have to stop by her spot on my way home. Something was off. I even hit up Takeya to see if she was free. But all she gave me was a rushed "hello" and some shit about being busy. I caught the attitude and heard her nigga in the background asking who was on the phone. I wasn't even tripping off of her flaky ass either. Maybe we'd never be close again. Some shit just ran its course.

I decided to go to the mall anyway despite going alone. Hell, I didn't mind. I really only fucked with my family or Brandi these days so being solo didn't sound bad anyway. I was feeling refreshed and good as hell with the pampering. I checked my reflection in the mirror. Putting on some of my Mac lipstick. The bright red color that contrasted my skin's smooth caramel brown complexion. Then adjusted my hair. Taking my high bun down and letting my fresh micros fall down my back. Running my hand through them to straighten them out.

I was rocking some light blue acid washed jeans. A tank top and a cropped grey hoodie since it was still cooler today. With my All white ones. My usual casual shit. I knew these jeans fit me just right hugging all of my curves in the right places. Making my ass pop even more than usual.

Walking around the mall, I took my time going into stores that I normally bypassed. Like the technology one and home goods. I only bought a few things. My last stop was Victories Secret. It was the one store I came in every time I went to the mall. I could never go without picking up at least one new thing.

Before I crossed to the other side of the isle to go in the store though, I stopped dead in my fucking tracks. Khalil was walking behind the same bitch that was pregnant by him. And the hoe looked beautiful with that pregnant glow. I couldn't even front. I turned to go in the opposite direction before the two saw me. His baby mama was talking to him and didn't see me. She was turned away looking at the display kiosk in the center of the isle, where the designer sunglasses were.

But King saw me. I wasn't lucky enough to catch a damn break. Our eyes met, and I skirted my gaze right in the opposite damn direction. Walking on the other side of where the couple was. That lump forming in my throat again. Not like the first time we reunited and I couldn't talk. This time filled with anger and sadness. I had to get the fuck out of here.

Khalil went back to tending to his bitch. Putting his arm around her and turning his attention all to her. I saw his actions through the corner of my vision. But kept facing forward, head held high and walked my ass past. Making sure to keep the same switch in my hips. Focusing only on my good ass energy. I knew I was beautiful in my own way and could pull any nigga I wanted. At least that's what I told myself these days. And right now I reminded myself of that. Even if Khalil chose his ex

101

over me. I was still that bitch. Fuck him. And fuck her.

I was out of here. Walking back towards the entrance to the mall where the food court was. I got an overwhelming craving for some Chinese once the smell hit my nose walking by. I had already kept my composure and dealt with seeing my ex and his little family. So there was nothing stopping me from getting something to eat. Nothing was going to fuck with my mood more than that shit.

I went over to the long ass line and waited. That's how bad I wanted some of the good smelling food. I took my phone out of my purse and started playing my word game on it. I didn't even notice the voice that called out until the older woman in front of me cleared her throat.

"Baby you better answer that man or we're all going to be waiting even longer for our food."

Having no clue as to what she meant. I looked up. And sure enough at the front of the line there was this good looking man standing there and instead of ordering he was staring right at me. Even though I was like five people back, it felt like there was no line between us. His eyes locked with mine and I couldn't look away even if I wanted to.

"Miss lady I got you. Come 'ere."

I turned my head side to side, looking behind me. Then pointed at myself to check and make sure this nigga was talking to me.

He was so good looking, well dressed in a suit. I wasn't sure if he meant me.

"Go on, hurry up. He's not ordering until you get up there."

I felt so awkward and the stares from the other customers could have burned a hole in me. But I walked my ass up to where the man stood and folded my arms across my chest not knowing how I should take his words or actions.

I couldn't front though, having a man take charge, look out for me, and call me to him was a turn on. I wasn't ready for anything serious or anything. But if a man wanted to pay for my lunch so what? There wasn't any harm in that. Plus I liked when a person went after what they wanted.

I was quiet as hell standing beside the stranger the whole time waiting for our food, after I told him to get me a beef lo mein. I didn't know his ass. He was sexy and the fact I even noticed that shit said a lot. When my eyes were for a nigga they were only for him. I didn't even look in another man's direction. But I was single again, so shit had changed. Even if my heart was still taken. I don't know if I'd ever fully get over Khalil. But he was out here happy and building his family.

That thought, the way this man was handling things and making me feel important was enough for me to agree to give him my number when he asked. I doubted he would call, and wasn't sweating it either way. I got lunch and a smile out of the encounter and that was enough.

I said a shy goodbye. He was smart enough not to try and cop a feel. The man's demeanor and way he dressed let me know he was paid. Not in a corny acting desperate way. Or a street way. He was different.

The rest of the afternoon, I thought back more on this past year than I wanted to. But it was time I really face facts and see shit for what it was. I was done with King and today just set that shit in stone. No sense feeling sorry for myself. That's just how life went sometimes. I still had a lot going for me.

After dropping off my things at my house, I left out early to stop by Brandi's spot before scooping Amyra up from daycare. Knowing that my friend needed me even if she didn't say it.

The minute I knocked on her door and she let me, I could tell she was going through it. Her pregnancy was showing more and more each time I saw her. Since she was in her last semester of cosmetology classes before she got her certificate, her advisor had given her an apprenticeship instead of taking the regular classes. So instead of having to go to the college 4 days of week, she went to her cousin's hair shop and put in only 2-3 days. Whatever she could manage.

When I say my friend was going through it. She was still dealing with morning sickness. But all times of the day and the shit hadn't started until a few weeks ago, later than it was supposed to. And she was sick around the damn clock.

Brandi always was on point. Hair, make up, clothes, all the way put together. But looking at her now, she was rough as hell. I felt bad for her.

"Hey sis, what you need me to do? You hungry?

"Now bitch you know my big ass is hungry. Don't even ask. I'm gon' eat whatever you cook for me. Too bad, it'll just come right back up though."

"We'll see. Maybe I can figure something out for you, so you can keep it down." I went into the kitchen and looked through her refrigerator.

Pulled out some ingredients and went to doing what I did best.

"I'm going to go ahead and get this started. Go pick up Amyra, then come back. You think Coup will be back to eat?" Brandi didn't say anything and there was a long ass pause. "Nope. Get to talking. What the hell's going on with ya'll. I thought you two were good. Let me find out that nigga did some dumb shit."

"Not him..." Brandi trailed off. "It's me. I'm the dumb one. I can't get my shit together. My head's all fucked up girl. I'm having a hard time accepting the fact that I'm about to be somebody's mother. I never wanted this." She opened her arms, looked down at her stomach.

As I stirred the marinade for the chicken I was making, I stopped what I was doing and looked right at my best friend in the eyes.

"I'm going to say this because I love you and I know you. You need to get some real answers from your mother before you bring this child into the world. You can't ignore your past B. You got to resolve that shit to move forward."

"What you mean answers? I'm good on my family situation. I just don't know if I'm cut out to be a mom. I don't feel that warm, fuzzy happy feeling. I don't feel the same connection. Not like Coup does. And he's not even trying to be around me right now because of it."

"Exactly! You don't know your own background. You don't understand your own parents or their love. So you're having a hard time connecting with your own unborn. You need answers. And I don't believe that shit for a second about not feeling a connection. You're just so used to blocking your feelings and not showing or being shown love that you haven't opened yourself up to the idea yet. But I know you and I know you already love your baby. Otherwise there would be NO baby."

Brandi didn't say anything else on the topic. It was how she always dealt with serious shit. She became quiet. It was about the only time she was quiet. Normally, Brandi was outgoing and talking shit about something. A hard exterior to the emotional woman she really was on the inside. Coup had gotten that side out of her more than I'd ever seen from her. I just hoped she took my advice and tried to get some peace on her own childhood. Otherwise she might block out the best thing to ever happen to her. Plus lose the man she loved. Coup was solid. But I couldn't even blame him for taking up for his seed. That was how he was supposed to move behind his child.

I picked up Amyra and came back to finish dinner. The meal was some banging ass baked chicken. I put fresh ginger in the marinade hoping it would do the trick with Brandi's stomach and the shit worked. She was able to keep everything she ate and drank down. We ended up falling asleep on the couch, laid out. With Amyra snuggled up on the floor. Wrapped in a blanket on a make shift pallet made out of pillows. The way she liked to do when she came over to Aunt B's.

Come morning, I woke up feeling refreshed like I got some of the best damn sleep I'd gotten in weeks. Better than sleeping in that empty ass bed all alone. And I was a wild ass sleeper.

I sat up on the couch. Looked around me and saw both Amyra and Brandi still asleep. Usually I'd get up and cook something. But I was feeling extra lazy this morning. Rolling onto my side I eased back down and wrapped the blanket around myself again. Enjoying the comfort while I pulled my phone off the charger.

When I unlocked it I saw that I had 2 new messages from when I was asleep. The first was from an unknown number so I looked at that one. It was from the man at the food court yesterday saying how he was thinking about my beautiful face and asking me to meet him today. I smiled, thinking about how I still had it. Yes, a bitch could pull a nigga. Lord knows break ups would have you questioning that shit. I didn't really feel the idea of linking up with a nigga that was basically a stranger. I went ahead and opened the other message. And of course it was from none other than fucking Khalil.

His message was short and to the point. "I miss you." That alone made me want to call his ass up, or drive over to wherever the hell he was and make things right. To fix things. But just as soon as I thought that, the reality hit me again. Nope, this nigga must've been drunk or something when he messaged me. Most likely in the middle of the night wanting some pussy. But that shit did not equal us having a happily every after. Especially when he had a bitch and a baby on the way.

Instead of hitting King back, I decided to go ahead and do some shit out of character. Knowing it was based on emotion, not rational thought, I responded to the mall nigga saying an "OK" that way I'd see what he was really talking about.

I set my phone back on the table and closed my eyes. Taking my ass back to sleep where my thoughts weren't consumed by the man I was trying to forget. I had to move the fuck on.

Khalil (King)

Fuck it, shit was moving along no matter what. That meant my head couldn't afford to be filled with wanting a bitch who didn't want to fuck with me. I wasn't with Rosaria. Wasn't doing a fucking thing except being a solid ass nigga for my seed. A fucking father's job. And the baby was coming in the next couple of months so it was shit I had to take care of out of necessity. To make sure he was set.

My own mother hustled better than most niggas to do her job plus my pops' who wasn't doing shit. Which is why no matter what the fuck was going on, the grind never fucking stopped for me. Business was business, work was work. A lot of niggas let pussy fuck with their paper. That would never be me. I put that shit on everything.

Heading over to my mommas to check in on her, I drove past our traps to see how traffic was looking. Our team handled their shit at the street level separate from us now. Except Coup. His ass stayed on them niggas. Applying pressure to make sure the packs kept moving. We hadn't seen any problems or competition since before Christmas. As far as I was concerned we were the only team in town.

Later today we were supposed to have a sit down with that dead mothafucka, D'Sean's, right hand to see if we could bring some niggas from the other side into the fold. It would make us get on a faster route to keep our hands clean with all the street level bullshit. That was the only fucking reason I was considering. Coup was the one directly gunned down by the opps and he was with having the meeting. He was really the one who was trying to bring the whole city together on some peace maker shit. I couldn't get into the same mindframe as him until I murked that nigga Demont period.

But I'd see what the fuck they were talking about. I had to respect my partna enough to let him run some things. And he was the one out here on the front lines a whole hell of a lot more than me.

I went into Lovely's expecting to see my mother like I usually did. In the kitchen cooking or on the couch smoking a port watching her shows and shit. But when I walked in my OG was getting ready to walk out. And she was dressed like she was going to meet somebody. Let me find out my momma had a new man in her life. That shit never fucking happened before. At fifty, she still looked young as hell. But the only thing my mother ever chased was bread. Not niggas. She was a real ass woman who held shit down on her own.

"Where you going ma?"

She sucked her teeth at me, "Now son you know to stay the fuck out of my business. I'm grown, grown in case you forgot. You the one I should be checking on? What's got you so fucked up you ain't come by in weeks?"

I caught the way she avoided my question. She was definitely up to some shit. She was dressed up in a new outfit, tight jeans and fresh air maxes. Looking at least 10 years younger. She was going some fucking where. But I would leave it alone for now. I couldn't say shit if she was happy. That was all that mattered to me anyway.

"I'm here now."

"Mmmhhhmmm. Well come by Sunday, I'm cooking and make sure you bring my baby and her momma."

I didn't answer, just nodded. Doing the same shit she did and ignoring what she was trying to get at.

Just as fast, my momma was out the door passing by me, telling me to lock up and shit. This was the first time I'd seen her out like this since I'd been home. I shrugged and kept it moving. Making a mental note to come by Sunday and get to the bottom of whatever the fuck she had going on. Me and Coup were past being on the rise. We were at the mothafucking top and I couldn't be too careful when it came to anyone connected to me, let alone close. Everybody was a potential target for the opps. The ones I knew about and the snake ass niggas I didn't know were gunning for us.

I drove out of the city. Headed to my new spot that was halfway between town and the new business across the border in South Carolina. It was a big ass house on 5 acres. Gated and away from nosy niggas and bitches. Nobody knew about this spot except for Coup. I upgraded thinking Imani and Amyra would be with me to fill up the halls and rooms and shit. Now when I came here it was to dip in and out for a second and then hit the road again.

111

Money never fucking stopped. So I showered, switched clothes and then headed back out in my Hellcat. I just copped a Bentley truck but this was my everyday whip. I drove listening to Moneybagg and then pulled into our main spot. These days, no weight was moving out of here. We used it as a place to meet up. Our shit had switched up so much. Now we had a new stash house closer to where I stayed outside of town. The shit was in a calm low key ass neighborhood. We were expanding on all fronts which meant we had to move like the fuck we had something to lose. I'm talking millions in a matter of months. There could be no fuck ups and Sergio wasn't a mothafucka I wanted to have a fuck up with.

After walking into the house, I spotted Coup already talking to that nigga Big Derek. The nigga who made it out alive the night we sprayed that bitch. He was blessed to still be breathing. He better use the fucking opportunity to do something with it. He wouldn't get another chance that was for damn sure.

I sat down in the chair on side of Coup. Across from the nigga and gave a head nod. Big Derek showed respect nodding back and addressing the shit that was the elephant in the room before continuing the conversation with Coup.

"I just want to clear the air. I'm a North side nigga. That's my hood and I'm always repping that bitch. But I never condoned the fuck shit my nigga was on. We didn't see eye to eye on a lot of shit. Towards the end I was ready to leave the whole operation and start out on my own. Loyalty was the reason I stayed. That was my mothafuckin' brother since the sandbox. So I ain't gon' come in here and disrespect him either."

"So why are you here then?" I asked.

"Like I was saying before you got here. It's time to make moves that's gon' put food on a nigga's plate. I want my team to eat and ya'll niggas the ones running things. I want us to work together. Leave the past in the past."

"Ain't no problem with working for us from your side? It won't cause problems for us?"

"It's been months now and we're over here starving. I'm not gon' lie and say there's no bad blood. You know this shit goes back. But niggas have to fall in line. It's the only way my side has a chance the way I see it. If mothafuckas push back, I'll handle it. It won't be ya'll problem. Leave that shit to me. But most my men are ready to work. Ready to stack some fucking paper. They're tired of the bullshit when it comes to feeding their families. And to keep it trill D'Sean wasn't looking out how he should towards the end."

I was hearing everything this nigga said and it all sounded good. But I didn't trust a nigga alive beside Coup.

"As soon as you hand us that nigga Demont then we can talk again, set some shit up. I hear where you're coming from. But you gotta understand this ain't no lil' boy shit my nigga. This here is the real fucking deal. Big time. And for us to even consider fucking with the side that's been the opps for a decade it's gotta be some sacrifices. That nigga touched my family and until then, ain't nothing more for us to discuss." I said flat out.

Big Derek looked at Coup and Coup nodded. "It's a small price for what this can do for your team. But it's up to you. We ain't gotta do a fucking thing for ya'll niggas. You think I give a fuck about the niggas who shot me? It might've been at D'Sean's order, but that don't mean a gotdamn thing. I always put money and respect before anything. Which is why you're even here nigga. This is a blood feud. And the only way it's gon' end is with that nigga dying. You're whole side is on shaky fucking ground. So I would take the deal if I were you."

Coup put his blunt out, stood up and ended the fucking conversation. I stood up along his side and Big Derek did the same. Knowing that his welcome was worn out now.

He walked towards the door and turned before leaving.

"You'll be hearing from me."

"Bet." Coup answered.

I'd already said my piece. Wasn't shit else to talk about until that nigga was delivered to me on a silver fucking platter.

When I left out, I felt one of my regular ass phones buzz. When I opened the shit up, it was a video message sent to my DM from some bitch I'd started fucking with since me and Imani was on the outs. I knew shorty thought I was back fucking with my ex Rosaria especially seeing us together out at the mall. But that wasn't the case. I only fucked one time since leaving the house that night as Imani's request. I never wanted to even fucking go. But I respected her enough to let her go and live the life she wanted even without me.

This hoe here knew what the fuck she was doing. Shorty was bad. A college girl by day and stripper by night. She was dark skin with Asian looking eyes and a fat ass. With some wet ass pussy. Since she'd gotten the dick she'd been tripping more and more. Forgetting that her place wasn't anything more than a fuck from time to time. I knew I was cutting her ass off. But not tonight.

I hit her up. Sending her a message back. I never gave ol' girl my number or no shit. But she could get this dick. I was back on my single shit. A heartless nigga that only wanted to fuck and then move the fuck on afterwards.

After I hit her up, she said she'd be ready when I pulled up in a few minutes. That's the sit I could fuck with. Without any fucking questions.

I pulled up and shorty walked out, wearing nothing but a long coat. When she sat down in the passenger seat, she took that shit off revealing she didn't have shit on underneath. Bare pussy, her pierced chocolate drop nipples sitting up right. Already hard. Good thing she kept the jacket under her ass, I didn't want my seats fucked up.

Not wasting any time, she leaned over confidently, trying to give me a kiss on the lips. Btu

I turned my mothafucking head and let her catch my jaw. I didn't know where this hoe's lips had been. She was butt ass naked in my whip ready to do whatever the fuck I wanted. It was no telling how many other niggas she had in rotation. And I didn't give a fuck. This wasn't nothing more than what it was.

It was pitch black outside, the rain just started and the neighborhood this hoe lived in was straight. Pretty quiet and shit, where I didn't have to worry about a nigga running up on me. Caught with my dick out.

"I missed you daddy."

"Oh yeah?"

She nodded, leaned further over and undid my jeans, pulled out my dick and licked her thick ass lips. Looked up at me and put those same lips around the head of my dick. Sucked and then came up. Ass in the air now, I reached up and set one hand on her fat ass and squeezed.

The bitched spit on my dick two times, nasty shit. Making it wet and then swallowed the mothafucka the best she could without choking. Went to work and sucking and slurping. Licked my balls and flicked her tongue back and forth. My dick was hard but the bitch wasn't making me cum from sucking my dick tonight. And her head was fire. Some of the best shit I ever had. I tried to get into the shit, but thoughts of Imani kept creeping in my head. Fucking up the feelings I should've been focused on instead. This was the first time I couldn't bust a nut off dome.

Shorty didn't seem to notice my mind was elsewhere and I wasn't into the shit she was doing. I lifted her head up by pulling her hair rough as shit. She liked that shit too.

She crawled over the center console and hopped on my dick, before I could pull out of fucking condom. I knew I was fucking up hitting raw, but it was done now and her pussy was gripping the fuck out of my shit. Fat, wet and tight. She might be a stripper but her pussy was A1. The girl got to fucking work again. Being anything but lazy, she held onto the damn steering wheel in front of her, put both her legs between mine and started riding my dick looking out the windshield like she was driving the gotdamn car instead of my dick driving her.

I slapped her ass when she came up hard as fuck that drove the bitch wild. She started bucking back against me, grinding her hips and popping her pussy. I felt her pussy tightening up and lifted her up some so she could get that shit out. Shorty kept still. Then fucked with the tip of my dick coming down real slow taking all my dick back inside her. Still gripping my shit and wetter than before. I reached around her front, stopped fucking around. Palmed her titties. Pressed down on them and held her all the way fucking down so she took all ten inches. She screamed out and started trying to get up and run from the dick. I fucked her slow and hard, deep inside. Then started tearing up her shit, using my hands to guide her body up and down the way I really wanted to fuck. So I could catch my

117

nut. When I felt that shit rising, I lifted her all the way up and finished jacking my dick. This bitch wasn't catching my kids. I'd already fucked up with Rosaria. The next woman who carried my seed would be my wife. And there was only one woman that I wanted to call my fucking wife.

Thoughts of Imani came back. I knew I was an even more fucked up nigga for fucking this girl, hitting raw and still thinking about my real woman. Shit was fucked up for us and who knew if it would ever change. But shorty still had my fucking heart whether we were together or not. It's just some shit you couldn't explain or change even if you wanted to. It was that real ass kind of love. That hood shit.

Imani

My first instinct was to dodge this nigga's message earlier, but after thoughts of Khalil and how he was moving on with his life, I gave in and responded. Now I was on my way to the restaurant we were supposed to meet at for dinner.

His name was Marcus and from asking Brandi about him neither one of us or anyone close to us knew anything about him. After talking to him a little bit more over the phone, he told me he was from Florida and new in town. Coming up to start a new business. He didn't say what type of business and I didn't ask. Shit wasn't serious enough for me to even care. It might sound bad but I knew I wasn't about to fall in love with the nigga. Not when King had my heart, lock and key. But he was a welcome distraction.

I wasn't a hoe so it wasn't like I had plans on fucking either. A good time is all I hoped for, but I wasn't expecting shit to be honest. The closer I got to downtown near where the restaurants were the more I was tempted to turn the fuck around and take my ass home. I'd never been out like this. Meeting a nigga like a single grown ass woman. But that was what I was now, like it or now.

When I arrived at the restaurant, I walked in and the hostess showed me to the table where Marcus was already waiting. I sat down. His smile brought one to my own face from the jump. He was easy on the eyes. All throughout dinner the conversation was okay, nothing special. It seemed like the man was fishing for information more than I was willing to give. I texted Brandi to let her know things were okay when I went to the bathroom. I looked at myself in the mirror.

On the outside, I looked the part. I was a fine ass bitch tonight in the outfit I picked out. It was that my inside didn't match. I was a mess. I felt broken and in that moment I wanted to run the fuck away. Thinking to myself, *"what the hell am I doing?"*. Why couldn't I just go home and call the only man I really wanted to talk to and be with? Me and King could work through this shit. Our love could get through anything. I walked back out of the bathroom with a renewed sense of confidence.

The date had been going okay. It just wasn't right. None of it felt 100% or genuine. Not on my part. I had already felt that swept off my feet feeling. And this nigga just wasn't it. It was no offense to him or anything.

I decided to make a graceful exit. By finishing the meal. Then thanking him for a nice night out and going home. Where I would pour my heart out the love of my life. The drink I had with dinner was still warm in my veins giving me the courage I needed to face this shit. At least mentally for now.

When I got back in the booth and sat across from Marcus, he seemed at ease and happy that I was back. I felt bad, I really did. But it was better not to string him along. There were two more new drinks and a cheesecake dessert on the table. With two forks for us to share the dessert.

"What's this?" I asked surprised.

"What can I say, I just wanted to end our dinner on the right note."

I nodded, and took a big ass drink from the second strawberry martini of the night. Not because this nigga was gaining points and I agreed with how he was feeling about our date. But because I knew I was about to piss him off. I was never one to hold back the truth. Even when it hurt.

"I gotta keep it real. You're a gentlemen and everything. Good company. It's just that I'm not really ready for this type of shit right now. To keep it real, I'm in love with someone else. And being here with you has reminded me of where I really want to be. I hope you find the right one for you. You seem like a good man."

"Damn. It's like that? Well I can't say I didn't figure you was taken. You're bad as hell. But I respect you keeping it a hundred. Let's just finish our drinks and then I'll walk you out."

"You ain't gotta do all that. I'm good. I'll pay for my food too."

"Nah baby, I'm not that type of nigga. You're good beau. I got you."

I didn't know why, but I felt like his attitude underneath the right words he was spitting had changed. It was in the stiffness of him movements and the look in his eyes changed too. Going from genuine to something else.

A feeling of wanting to get the fuck away from him came over me. For no real reason. Not other than me coming clean and telling him straight to his face that he wasn't the nigga I was thinking about or wanting to be here with. I knew that shit probably hurt his pride even if he didn't admit it. He was a man after all and pride was a big thing to any nigga.

I hurried the fuck up and gulped down the rest of my drink. Not taking a single bite of the cheesecake and neither did Marcus. He didn't finish his drink, but true to his word he took care of the check and laid down some bills to take care of the meal plus the tip. I meant the shit I said to him though. I didn't wish nothing but good on this man for his future.

We walked out of the restaurant together, him behind me. And I made sure to keep two feet ahead so our bodies didn't come in contact or anything. For some reason, by the time I made it to the front of the building and opened the glass door, my head felt funny as hell. I got dizzy as the liquor started kicking in more. I guess I had become a lightweight, not really drinking in a minute. The two drinks seemed to be doing more than a little bit.

Marcus came up behind me, put his arm on my back to offer support.

"I'm good... I just..." I lost my train of thought and stumbled.

My heel caught in the cracks between the cement in the sidewalk. I looked straight ahead and everything began to move. My vision was fucked up. Marcus held my arm. Taking on the brunt of my weight. My head felt fuzzy and I knew I was more messed up then I'd ever been.

"Yeah, that's right. I got you now." This nigga said like he was proud of some shit.

Everything clicked for me. I was drugged. I began to panic and tried to run. But my head and body weren't working right. When I thought "run" I actually fell to the ground. Marcus stood over me with his hand out for me to take with a big ass grin on his face. And that's when my vision blacked out and I stopped thinking altogether.

Only feeling anger and fear overcoming the little bit of coherent thoughts I had. Before those stopped too.

Brandi

With Coup not fucking with me and my due date getting closer and closer. The feeling of being in this shit all alone was getting the best of me. I knew it had to do with how I came up and how I didn't ever feel like I could count on anybody but my damn self that was making this shit worse for me. I'd finally opened my heart. I'm talking all the way, and became vulnerable. And where did that get me? Laying around day in day out, crying my eyes out. Talking shit the whole time to myself about being weak for a man. Some shit I swore against. But these pregnancy hormones were no joke.

I decided that today was the day that I would go talk to my momma though. I doubted she gave any real answers to my questions. But both Coup and now Imani kept talking about how I needed answers.

So fuck it, I'd see what Denise had to say. That was my mother's name. And that's what I actually called her. I'd been the real mother for a long ass time as far as finances and taking care of my brothers and sisters went. I was still going over to the house twice a week when they got out of school to check their schoolwork and make sure they were straight with clean clothes and food in the fridge. Luckily my brothers were old enough to look out for themselves now for the most part. But at least they never had to worry about a meal.

124

I didn't admit this shit to anyone. Not even Imani fully, but my mother was a straight up junkie at this point. Any stamps she got, when back in the streets to feed her habit. She wasn't this bad when I was younger. But as I got older, some shit changed. And everything about her way of living and attitude about her own children and life got worse. That's why I stepped up and looked out for my siblings the way I did.

The minute I walked in the door, I was ready to turn back around and take my ass home. Already regretting this shit. But Denise spotted me before I got the chance to turn the fuck around.

"Uh, look who decided to grace us with her presence today." She slurred with a cigarette hanging out of the side of her mouth.

Throwing her arms out like she had a damn audience, but the only one in the room was my littlest sister. Who was sitting on the couch watching something on the TV.

"What's up Meka?"

My sister got up quick, ran over to me and hugged my body. Throwing her arms around my waist. Meka was getting taller each time I saw her. She was 11 now and I made a mental note to take her out shopping in the next week. The clothes she had on were looking like she was half grown out of them. That shit made me feel like I was slacking on my responsibilities.

"I missed you." She exclaimed.

"I missed you too. Us grown folks is about to talk, so go in your room for a minute. I'll come back there before I leave."

"You're not staying for dinner?"

I hadn't planned on it, so I let her down gently since she sounded so disappointed. I hated that shit.

"I'm gon' start it for you. But I gotta get back home today. But I tell you what, I'll come by Tuesday after you get out of school. I'm taking you shopping. How does that sound?"

Now she was smiling, walking towards her room like I told her to.

"OK. I got to do some make up work anyway."

"And you better, don't let me find out your grades are slipping!" I called behind her.

I was proud that she knew I would be on her ass if she didn't get on those damn books. I'm glad I came over. I was wondering where the rest of my family was though. The 4 brothers that seemed to be gone more and more every time I stopped through. The next youngest one was 14 and he was following right behind the others. As much as I wanted better for them, than to be out in the streets getting it how they lived. I understood that they had to do what they had to do to survive. It was a cold ass world.

If I had more ends then I would be able to take care of them. And they wouldn't have to be out risking their lives. I needed to talk to them this week when I came back. If none of them were around, I'd go out and find their asses to see how they were doing personally. Instead of hearing it from Meka. I needed to see for myself.

"You think you can come by here and get her hopes up, just to leave again and go live that fancy life of yours. With that man of yours."

I ignored the baiting that Denise was doing. Trying to make me feel guilty for her fucking responsibilities. She could see I was pregnant now, and instead of asking me how I was doing, her oldest fucking daughter, she didn't say shit on the subject. She was and always had been selfish as hell. Only able to feel sorry for herself instead of worrying about her damn kids. She didn't really give a fuck about any of us. And now that I was carrying my own, her sins was affecting my own mentality.

I went ahead and got to the point of why I came over to deal with her ass anyway.
She huffed and puffed, than sat down at the kitchen table. Still being over the top dramatic dropping into the seat. Causing all kind of unnecessary noises.

I went into the small adjoining kitchen and pulled out some chicken to thaw in the sink. Along with the other food I'd bought a couple weeks ago that I'd need for sides to go with the dinner I was getting started for Meka and my hard headed ass brothers whenever they finally made it home. We were a dysfunctional ass family, but I wouldn't trade my sister or brothers for anything else in the world. I even loved Denise, even though she didn't deserve it.

"I wanna ask you something."

"Well I'm here ain't I? What are you waiting for?" She lit another cigarette.

"It's about my father. I want to know who he is, so I can know where I come from. It's been a lot of shit on my mind and it always comes back to not knowing why he never wanted anything to do with me. All you told me was he found out you were pregnant and you never heard from him again. But you never told me who he was. You never told me anything about him at all. I'm just trying to put some pieces together so I can make sure I'm ready to be the mother I need to be."

"I don't see what that man has to do with you having a baby. You should be worried about how you're gonna keep that man instead of that baby anyway. They always leave afterwards. You're dumb as hell if you think any different."

I felt my anger getting the best of me. I was ready to tell my mother off and really giver her a piece of my mind. But one thing about me, no matter how fucked up she was and how much she fucked up with her children. I never got disrespectful. The only shit that came close was me calling her by her government instead of mom. But I couldn't give her a title she didn't rightfully earn. To me she was Denise period.

"Can't you for once just keep it real with me? Damn, is it that hard? Just tell me something, Anything!" My voice got louder, and I turned and looked her dead in the face. Hands on the countertop pressed against it with all the aggression I felt but couldn't take out on her.

"His name is Thomas Johnson. And his no good ass has a whole family. He didn't want nothing to do with me or you. You can bet he still doesn't. I don't know why you want to dig up old bones. But I hope you're ready to find out the truth."

"What does that mean?"

"Just like I said. You sure you want to go down this path?"

I nodded my head.

"Alright, well I'll tell you then since you're grown now and think you know every damn thing. That man lied to me to get me in bed every chance he got. I was only 16 years old and he was 32. Already married with children. But my dumb young ass didn't know any better. So when this good looking black man promised me the world I believed him. He had the looks, a good job. Was successful and everything. It never occurred to me that he was using me. And that he was the one fucked up in the head. By the time I found out I was pregnant, of course I went to him all happy. Thinking we would be a little happy family." My mother laughed and flicked her cigarette butt. Taking her time to keep on going. Inhaling a deep pull and breathing out the smoke again. "Well, you already know that shit didn't happen. He had other plans, He wanted me to get an abortion. He drove me to the place and everything. Handed me $1000, told me to "get the fuck out of his car". His exact words. And never call him again. That I was a big mistake and he didn't want anything to do with my young ass anymore.

"So you didn't go through with it."

"No shit? I guess not..." She said sarcastically. But I let that shit go. "Well I stood there for damn near an hour crying my eyes out. And clinging to the buy off bills that he handed me. Like they would make me feel better. I thought about going through with it, but I couldn't let go of the possibility of him changing his mind. Of our baby bringing us back together. Maybe he was just mad for the time. Anyway, I walked all the way home. The rest is history. I had you. He never called, never came by. Didn't give a fuck. It was the way he wanted it. So what could I do?"

"You never saw him again? He never tried to see me?" I questioned. Not wanting to believe that my father didn't even have the heart and wasn't man enough to give a fuck about this own daughter.

My mother shook her head no. "Bt when you were around 5 or 6 I got up enough guts to go take you to see him. We took the bus and then got off near his house. He'd lived in the same house since he first started seeing me. He even took me there when his wife and kids were out of town a couple times. When he was messing with me. So I walked right up to the front door, with you holding my hand. I was going to make him face both of us. Well... it turned out his wife answered and her daughter was right by her side like you were me. She gave me one look and then closed the door in

130

my face. I banged and banged on the door. Until finally Thomas opened it back up. He told me that he wanted nothing to do with me or you. That he hadn't changed his mind and that as far as he was concerned you were an orphan from the day you were born. That I should have gotten the abortion. So you see that man never wanted to be in your life. He didn't want me or you. It was all a game to him."

I had tears streaming down my face by the time she was done with her last words. Every word she told me stung to the core. I was at loss for words but I needed more.

"So I have a sister?"

"Mmmhhhmm. And like I said don't expect nothing from that either. These people didn't want nothing to do with either of us. Blood didn't matter then, it won't matter now. Mark my words."

With that I ended the conversation. Turned back around so she couldn't see how much the shit affected me. Wiped away my tears with the back of my hands, then went back to starting dinner. Trying to get the fuck out of here as fast as I could. Pregnancy made me emotional enough. And now hearing the truth of it all, didn't help in the least.

After I had the food in the oven and on the stove. I went and said my goodbyes to Meka and told her to finish the dinner for me. She showed me her schoolwork that she just finished and I left. With a heavier heart than I came with. Already knowing my next steps were going to be finding my deadbeat ass father.

Imani

I woke up with my clothes off, lying face down naked. My head was pounding and I felt sore all over. I scanned the room trying to make sense of last night. That only made the pain worse. I sat up, rubbing my temples trying to ease the pain. Then looked around for my clothes in what I figured was a rundown hotel room. Nothing looked familiar.

Trying to think back to last night, the final thing I remembered was leaving the restaurant with Marcus and then realizing I was drugged. That was the last fucking thing I could think of. I went to cover myself up quick as hell in case him or some other niggas came in the room or planned to come back. I had to get the fuck out of here fast.

When I stood up a shooting pain went through my thighs and my pussy hurt. Like it never did before. I hurried up into the bathroom. On the way I saw my clothes laying on the floor like they'd been thrown off by somebody. I couldn't remember shit so there was no telling. A feeling of fear came over me worse than it did after the shit with Demont.

I tried to use the bathroom, but I couldn't even pee. The pain when I pushed let me know that what I feared was most likely true. I'd been raped. I finished, then stood up, rushing to put my clothes from the date back on. But the more I moved around, bending and pulling the items over my body, the more soreness all over I felt. I went ahead and quickly looked at my face in the mirror, fixed my braids the best I could wrapping them into a bun without a hair tie. Dark circles from smeared mascara were around my eyes. There was a deep red bruise on my jaw like I'd been punched in it. And sure enough when I touched it, it hurt like hell. Just like the rest of my body.

I shook my head at myself. I should've known better, was all I could think. Deep regret started to take over my thoughts. But I shook them away. The fear of that nigga or whoever else coming back motivated me. I basically ran the fuck out of the hotel.

Around the block, I stopped for a minute. I didn't have a car but I had my purse at least. So I looked inside hoping I wasn't robbed along with the other shit that happened to me. Luckily all my shit seemed to be in place. Even my phone, but it was turned off. When I powered it on, I saw that it still had 50% charge. I walked further away from the hotel. And saw some recognizable shit. Realizing where I was so I could get home.

So I hurried the hell up and called Brandi. She picked up and told me she was over this way and would be to the spot I told her I was standing at. Giving her the intersection a couple blocks up, where I'd walked while on the phone.

When she pulled up to the sidewalk, I hurried the hell up and got in her car. She waited a few minutes until we crossed over to our side of town before saying a single word. But the tension in the air was thick as hell.

"What the fuck happened to you?"

"I went out on a date last night like I texted you. Shit was good, I thought. I ended it early and planned to go home because I was missing King. I didn't want nobody else but him. Next thing I know I'm walking out of the restaurant headed to my car and I started feeling fucked up. Stumbling and shit. That nigga Marcus was right there when I fell. I remember him saying some funny ass shit to me and thinking he drugged me. Then that was it. I blacked out I guess. After that I don't remember a single fucking thing. Until I woke up naked in a hotel room this morning. Hurt, sore, and feeling sick. I couldn't even pee." I started crying.

Sobbing, body shaking. I'd been through a lot of different shit, but this topped the list as the most fucked up.

"It's gonna be okay. You're safe now. I'm taking you to the hospital."

"NO!!! Just take me home. I just want to take a bath and go to sleep in my bed. And forget any of this happened."

"Are you sure?" Brandi questioned, sounding hesitant.

"Please, that's all I want!"

And my best friend dropped the subject. Normally, we'd be talking up a storm. But I couldn't. Everything hurt. I was mentally and physically exhausted. I fell asleep leaning against the window before we made it to my house. Brandi shook me awake, then tried to come in with me. But I refused more of her help. I didn't want any company right now. I just wanted to be alone.

Showered and sleeping. I'd get Amyra later, when I woke up.

That's exactly what I did too. I showered, washed my body from head to toe until the hot water ran out. Sitting on the floor of the shower letting the steaming hot water run over me. While I cried my eyes out. Then when it turned cold, I got out, wrapped myself in a towel and fell asleep in my bed. The one safe place I had left. It was hours, I don't know how many before I woke up to a shooting pain in my lower stomach. I clutched myself with my hands. Then I felt the blood come. Soaking the sheets beneath me.

I knew right away I was having a miscarriage. And the worst part is I didn't even know I was pregnant. I picked up my cell, laying as still as possible. While pain took over my body. I screamed out, but no one could hear. It was dark outside now from the darkness that filled my room. I had been asleep for a long ass time and had a bunch of missed calls. One of them from Khalil. I hit send next to his name knowing I needed help.

"I'm having a miscarriage. Can you come get me? I need to go to the hospital." I whispered, trying to move as little as possible. Breathing lighter to stop the excruciating pain I was experiencing.

"What the fuck you say? Where you at?!"

"Home."

"I'm on the way shorty. Stay on the phone with me."

"It hurts so bad."

"I'm coming. I got you."

"Thanks."

Then there was silence on our line. I didn't want to talk because the shit really did hurt every time I said something. On top of the pain I was in from who knows what the fuck happened to me. Now I was going through losing a child, I didn't even know I was carrying. The tears started back. I kept as silent as I could so King wouldn't hear though.

A few minutes later, I heard footsteps coming down the hall towards the room and King speak into the phone along with his voice inside the house.

"I'm here bae."

He hung up and I let the phone fall on the bed next to me away from my ear. Khalil came into the bedroom hurrying up. I felt myself getting light headed and feeling overwhelmed tired. Like I hadn't slept in days.

Next thing I knew the love of my life was talking shit to me as he lifted me in his arms. Scooping me up and cradling me. I could hardly keep my eyes open.

"You better not fuckin' do this to me."

"Mmmm." I barely got out.

I wanted to say so much more back, but I couldn't.

Waking up with the same feeling of dread I had in the hotel room just a day before was shattering to my soul. Then remembering last night. The pain, the blood, calling King and the miscarriage, I started balling crying again. This shit hurt more than my body. I lost a child. Just as I started covering my face with my hands to catch the tears, the hospital door to my room opened.

Khalil was walking in with Coup and Brandi right behind him. Along with Lovely holding Amyra's hand. I forced myself to just as quick wipe the tears away and put on a smile for my daughter. She didn't need to be worried about her momma. She needed to live in her innocence as long as possible.

"Mommy! Mommy!"

I reached my hand down for her to take. Then wrapped it around her shoulders. I was still sore as a mothafucka but I didn't show that shit a bit.

"Okay baby, let's' go see what they got in that store we passed on the way. How does that sound?" Lovely said to her calmly.

"Okay, can we get something for mommy?" I heard her say as she was walking right back out the same door she just came in.

That shit made me get all emotional again. But I held back the tears at least.

"How are you doing sis? You had us so damn worried. I knew I should've brought your ass straight here when I picked you up." Brandi came to my side and hugged me as close as she could.

"What you mean you should've brought her here?" King's voice cut through the moment that we were having.

Brandi leaned back and gave me a regretful look, like she knew she fucked up saying too much. But it was okay at this point. Khalil would find out sooner or later. I wasn't telling him details anyway, I couldn't even if I wanted to.

No sooner than when I looked up on the other side of the bed and made eye contact with Khalil, Brandi was finding an excuse to get up out of the hospital room with Coup. Practically dragging his ass. So by the time I took a deep breath, inhaling the clean hospital air to keep my nerves straight, I was all alone to tell King this shit face to face. I already knew he was going to be pissed.

"There's something I need to tell you..." Khalil didn't budge. Not saying anything to my lead. He kept his eyes locked on mine. His expression already looked like he wanted to strangle my ass. If I wasn't laying here already he might have put me here anyway. I kept going, "I went out on a date last night."

"The nigga you was fucking did this? I see the bruises and shit. You let some nigga beat your ass and kill my fucking seed!" Khalil yelled at me.

This was the other side of the nigga I loved. The street side. I heard it in his voice. He was ready to kill my ass if I gave the wrong answer. As outraged as I felt that he thought I was that dumb to put myself fin a position to be fucking with a nigga like that willingly hurt. But I did give this nigga Marcus opportunity even if I didn't mean to. That shit was on me and there was nothing I could do about the shit.

"I wasn't fucking him. It was our first date. You got to believe me, I didn't want none of this to happen. I didn't want to lose our child. This shit hurts worse than you could possibly understand."

I had been strong up to this point. But seeing the man you love stare at you with hate broke my spirit more than it was. Here, I'd lost my memory of last night, was pretty sure I'd been violated and then lost my baby that I didn't know I was carrying. But damn, I was a good ass mother and this loss hurt. I loved my baby even if it was only temporary. That life was a part of me. Khalil just didn't understand. And I wasn't looking for his pity but he should be able to hear me out at least. Right now his own hurt wasn't letting a single word I said get through to him. He believed what he wanted to believe. There was no sense trying.

Just then a buzzing noise came from over by the cushioned windowsill seat in the hospital room. Khalil went over, dug inside and pulled out my phone. I guess somebody took the time to pack me a bag. Probably Brandi, since she always looked out.

Khalil looked down at the screen then tossed the phone on my bed.

"Yeah, you're on some bullshit for real. I don't know what kind of games you're playing. But as far as I'm concerned your dead to me. This was a message from God shorty. You couldn't even carry my seed without fucking another nigga and costing my child's life. I don't want nothing to do with yo' ass. Real talk. I'm out."

"Khalil! Khalil, why are you doing this to me?!" I yelled after him

When I looked down at my phone and unlocked it I lost all rational thought and control of myself. There in a video message was the nigga Marcus raping me while I was unconscious. I was laid out, face down and he was staring in the camera smiling. Fucking the shit out me while I was passed out. Unless you knew that I was drugged you might think it was consensual. But this shit was like watching some of the worst shit you could see. I couldn't even finish watching. I didn't even want to know anymore what he did to me.

I threw the phone and screamed. My breath caught in my chest. Before I started hyperventilating. Making the machines buzz and beep loud as hell. It didn't faze me though. I kept screaming between heaving trying to get enough air. My chest feeling like it was going to burst. The nurses came running in after King was gone. I couldn't focus, couldn't think straight. My heart, mind, body and soul were broken. I couldn't even catch my breath. There was nothing left for me. I felt like I had lost everything. I didn't want to be alive anymore.

So when the nurses stuck a needle in my arm, injecting me with something, I didn't give a fuck. Finally, the calm I wanted took over me.

Khalil (King)

A nigga was fucked up behind this shit. I had lost the baby with Imani and to me that shit turned my heart cold as fuck towards her. There was nothing else to say to her. I couldn't even look at her hoe ass. She was lucky I didn't put a bullet in her chest for how my heart broke behind the bullshit she was on. First she kicked my ass out like I was nothing to her. And I still had the mind to fuck with her even though she didn't want to hold me down for shit that came before her. That was some weak shit if you asked me.

I needed a solid ass woman in my corner. Especially with where I was at in the game now. Not a fucking headache and a sneaky bitch that I couldn't trust. It never even crossed my mind that Imani was like that. But the truth was right in my gotdamn face. I felt like a fucking pushover, getting played out here. And my enemies were probably sitting back loving the shit.

At least I was bout to get some good fucking news today. It was just after eleven at night. I hadn't talked to any mothafuckas since leaving the hospital. Not even Coup. I had to get my head right. I sat in my big ass office in the new house. Smoking backwood after backwood. Trying to keep from going to murder this bitch. Going over paperwork from the arcade. But none of the numbers were even registering in my fucking brain right now. Then Coup hit the business line with a message about "good news".

141

That shit was hopefully the one thing I'd been waiting on.

I pulled into our new stash house, which was outside the city only about 10 minutes from my new property. It was right in the middle of a fucking field. Hidden behind a band of tall pine trees and overgrown brush. The single driveway was the only way in and out. The spot had a big ass building out back that was almost the same size as the main house. And behind that was a fucking barn. The place came with stalls and shit for animals.

I hadn't been out here in a month. Not since we paid the cash for it and moved the safes and some extra product out here. It wasn't a property that stood out as special but it was perfect for the shit we were into.

I made it there and was met by a fucking all white cargo van, pulled next to building out back. The bitch looked suspicious as a mothafucka. So I hit Coup up, who told me shit was a GO. I went ahead and parked. Then walked inside the building where he said he was at. After opening the door, I saw my nigga wasn't fucking lying when he said "good news". About the only thing that could bring me some fucking peace today.

It was about time that this shit was over. What better day than today to kill this fuck nigga Demont.

The nigga was tied up to a chair in the back of the building by a work table. Coup already had shit set up. The toolbox was out and ready to use.

No more looking for this nigga. And there wasn't going to be any talking. He was a dead man.

"Look, I ain't mean no..."

I came up and swung on the bitch nigga. Hitting him straight on the jaw and busting his shit wide open. I didn't stop there. All the fucking anger and rage from these past months down to today was coming out on this nigga's face. Blow after blow bringing more blood. But I didn't give a fuck. He picked the wrong one to fuck with. By the time I finished the nigga's face wasn't even recognizable. My knuckles were fucked up, my adrenalin on a hundred so I didn't feel any of it.

"I don't want to hear shit you got to say nigga."

Coup leaned against the work table, blunt hanging out his mouth and picked up the extended handle sludge hammer.

"Here."

"My nigga. That's what I'm talking 'bout." I grinned and took the tool out of his hand.

Then walked back over to Demont. Damn sure not listening to his pleas and begging shit. All I saw was red. I needed to make him pay for even thinking he could come against me and survive. Let alone the months he was hiding out. I swung all the way back and then came down straight on his knee cap with full force. The minute there was impact, a loud ass cracking sound echoed through the room. The nigga's knee cap shattered from a single blow. So I went for his other leg.

"AHHHHHHHHHHH! AHHHHHHHHHH! AHHHHHHHHHHH!" The nigga kept fucking screaming.

It wasn't even worth hearing the shit no more. I pulled my new FN out. Holding it at my side. The tool in one hand and pistol in the other.

"Nigga you look ready to go to war. Where the fuck you goin'?" Coup laughed, cracking jokes now like only my cousin could with is high ass.

"Fuck you nigga. I'm ready to kill this nigga and get this shit over with. His bitch ass screaming like a lil' ass girl and shit."

"Yeah, you right. I ain't never heard a scream from a nigga that loud or high. Like he singing for help."

"W-A-I-T! I... can help... you..." He struggled to get out. Realizing he was really about to die.

"How?"

If there was more shit I needed to know, now was his time to talk. It wasn't changing his fate. But he didn't know that.

"You'll let me live? I mean... Ahhhhh. Fuck... I didn't do nothing..."

"Nigga you better get to talking, or forever hold yo' peace!"

"O-kay. There's another nigga after you. And he already got to Imani. I didn't... know... he was gon'..."

"Where's he at!?" I interrupted his slow ass attempt at saving his life. The shit he said pissed me off even more if possible. I knew the shit he was speaking on had to do with me having to just leave

144

from the fucking hospital after losing my seed. If I wasn't seeing red before, that's all I fucking saw now.

"I don't know!... But he's from Florida. He came up last week. His people stay on your side."

I went ahead, held my gun up two feet from Demont's dome and fired. His shit split open on impact. Some of the blood splattered on my arm and shirt. The nigga's body slumped over, brains blowed out. Exactly what the fuck he deserved for the lame shit he pulled with Imani and for coming at our side to begin with. It was another threat out the damn way. And the next one was still out there apparently.

I thought I'd feel relieved. But I couldn't even enjoy this nigga not being a thorn in my fucking side because there was more unfinished business when it came to my family.

"Follow me." Coup interrupted my thoughts.

I nodded and tucked my gun back in my waistband, then took off the hoodie I had on, and walked out the way Coup was. He went around to the back part of the building. Over to the barn which was a few hundred yards back. Inside there were about a dozen or so hogs. The mothafuckas were loud as fuck and big as shit.

"Damn bruh, what you been out here doing? These mothafuckas big as shit. What the hell you feed them? And they smell like shit too. I know you got something up your sleeve."

"These are the clean up crew. It takes 3 pigs 15 minutes on average to eat an entire fucking

145

body. From head to toe, bone and all. No fucking trace of remains when they're through."

"You serious?"

"Dead ass nigga. Last time Sergio came down here he made a comment 'bout the shit when you was in the back of the arcade handling the weight. I asked him if it was true and he vouched for the mothafuckas. Swore up and down on it. Even extended an invitation for me to fly down to Columbia and shit to see. I left it at that though. He wasn't 'bout to prove shit to me and me be the fucking dummy that loses his life. I mean the niggas cool but it's something off."

"With Sergio? Nah, he's straight. A little different but that shit gotta come with the territory bruh. He's 8 generations in this shit. So what you're saying is these mothafuckin' pigs 'bout to do all our clean up work for us? I got to see this shit."

"Aight, let's get the nigga and see. I say since there's so many of 'em that it won't even take 5 minutes. What you say?"

"We gon' see what you're talkin' bout."

And the nigga wasn't lying. It wasn't 5 minutes more like 10. But those hogs were the fucking truth. They tore the body up. And nothing was left. Not even the fucking clothes. Shit was sick as hell to watch. We both ended up leaving them to it, while Coup showed me around and told me more about what he wanted to add to the property out here. He was a visionary like me so I could fuck with all his ideas. This shit was a partnership all the way.

After leaving the spot I thought about heading home but decided against it. Fuck it, I was all the way out here now. I might as well go by Rosaria's then the arcade. And after that I was hitting up the strip club or some shit tonight. Turning all the way up.

Brandi

I had been so damn close to going to my father's house the shit was scary. But then I got a phone call from Imani and I made a U-Turn to go pick her up. I took it as a sign that it wasn't meant to be. But that was over a week ago. Shit had settled down for the most part with my best friend, I had my emotions in check even with Coup still staying away.

That was the fucked up part. He was all nonchalant like being away from me didn't matter either way to him. So I did the exact same thing when I saw him at the hospital. Don't get me wrong, we ended up fucking right there in the parking deck in the backseat of his old school car. Even pregnant, and showing bad I needed some dick. And being around him had me wet from the jump. So it was on sight.

I guess technically we had been fucking around ever since. But it wasn't the same as being together. Living together. Laying in bed together. All the shit I never wanted to come to depend on that I was now missing.

Today I was determined to go through with my plan, make shit happen and introduce myself to my father. As nervous as I should be, for the most part I just wanted to get it the fuck over with so I could get my man back. It sounded petty but that's where my heart was at. I never wanted to be a needy bitch, but I needed me some Coup even if I acted like I didn't. And maybe him and Imani were right, this was what I needed to face. Then I could put the shit behind me and open myself up. Warm up to being a mother. Something had to give, that shit was for certain.

I pulled up to the street that his house was supposed to be on. It was familiar as hell. I knew the area well. It was where Takeya lived. I went ahead and put the address in my GPS on my phone and then hit the button for directions on the map. Set my phone on the passenger seat and started listening to the directions over the Bluetooth. As I got closer each turn was like déjà vu. The directions took me the same way I drove to one of my best friend's house.

I didn't think anything of it until the voice from the GPS said the destination was right on my left side. I pulled up to curb and couldn't believe my fucking eyes. I was looking right at Takeya's house. This shit had to be a mistake. Or I hoped it was. I double checked the address. Never having paid attention to the actual street numbers before when I came here to pick her up.

Sure enough the numbers I put in the GPS matched the ones on the text from my mother. The one I went back and convinced her to give. After hours of listening to her bullshit.

I guess it was possible that my father didn't live here anymore. Maybe that explained the coincidence. I was getting ready to pull off from the side of the curb when a man came out of the front door and walked over to the white jeep parked in the driveway. I'd never seen Takeya's family before the more I thought on it. But the minute I laid eyes on the man I knew he was my father. He had my same eye shape and the way they were set on his face was identical to mine. It was the one feature that was distinct about me, different than any of my brothers or sister.

I was far from a scary bitch, so I got my ass out of the car and slammed the door behind myself. I was hot. Mad as hell and my adrenalin was pumping from the second I realized this man was in fact the man who didn't want shit to do with me. He thought he could fuck a young girl, fuck up her life and then say fuck the child he gave life to. My blood was boiling by the time I stepped to his car. He was already inside with the engine running, ready to back out.

I knocked on the damn window of his shit to get his attention. He rolled down the window,

"Can I help you?"

"Yes actually you can. Is your name Thomas Johnson?

"Why are you asking? What's this all about?" He asked looking more skeptical.

"Just answer the question please. Is your name Thomas Johnson or not?" I had an attitude. But damn I didn't give a fuck. It was a simple question. I'd go on my way leave his ass alone if he wasn't who I was looking for.

He gave a quick head nod indicating "yes" that was his name. Fuck! I thought.

"Do you know Denise?"

And that was the only shit I needed to say to this man. His eyes flashed with recognition and he looked like a scared little ass boy. I couldn't even make up how worried he looked. All that bass in his voice questioning me a minute ago was gone now. It was all cap.

"Look I don't want any problems. I know what this is about. You think you've found something here. But you're wrong. I'm not who you think I am. And let me guess you're here because you need some money. The apple doesn't fall far from the tree I see."

"Oh no? So you're not my sperm donor. The sick man who wanted to fuck on a young thing and then knocked her ass up and left her. The man who turned his back on his own seed? That's not you?"

"You got it all wrong. I never wanted children. Especially not a... biracial one. Like I said you got it all wrong. Denise seduced me and then lied to me about keeping the baby. I gave her money and told her that I'd sign over my rights. I don't have any children outside of my marriage. Do you understand?"

"Yeah I understand exactly what type of man you are. Your ass doesn't have to worry about me after today, I'll tell you that shit. But let me ask you one more question. Do you have a daughter named Takeya?"

He squinted his eyes. "How do you know that?"

And with that answer I chucked up the deuces and turned on my fucking heel. I swear this man was lucky I was pregnant and keeping myself calmer than I used to. I had the mind to fuck up his jeep that's how mad I was. More for my mother than for myself. She was fucked up in a lot of ways but knowing her story from when she had me to now, made me see her in a different light. She was far from perfect but she chose to keep me when everything in the world and everyone didn't want her to.

So where she fell short as parent at least her love was enough to bring me into this world. She was just a kid herself, having a kid. No wonder why she was all fucked up in the head.

I got back in my car and headed home. Sent Coup a message telling him to come through when he wasn't busy. I didn't know if he wanted to be back with me as much as I wanted him. But the peace I'd been seeking with becoming a mother myself finally made sense now.

Now the other shit about Takeya. I was on her ass tomorrow after I filled Imani in on the bullshit. I was taking her to lunch, trying to get her out of the house since she was still having a hard time with everything. Maybe this would take the focus off of her situation at least. But best believe I was getting to the bottom of things.

I was surprised when I pulled into the yard to see Coup's truck already parked and waiting on me. I hurried up moving faster than usual. The extra weight from my baby bump not holding me up. I was still comfortable. Pregnancy wasn't that bad after all.

When I stepped inside I was surprised as hell. Rose petals lined the floor, making a path down the hall to the bedroom. I followed them. Not fully believing Coup was behind this shit. Don't get me wrong, he was the type of nigga to take care of me. But this romantic shit wasn't him. His way of being romantic was handing me stacks of money.

Sure enough once I hit the bedroom and opened the door, he was coming out of the bathroom.

"What's all this?"

"I know that I've been gone a minute and things have been rough on you. Real shit, I shouldn't have left when you. I had you out here alone carrying my seed. But I'm here now and I ain't goin' nowhere. You're the woman for me."

"Bae, I'm the one who's sorry. My head's been fucked up. But I met my father today and you were right. I feel a weight lifted off of me. I don't want to be like his ass. I want to give our daughter the best of everything. You ain't gotta worry anymore. I love this little girl too."

"You serious?"

"Yes, bae and believe me after meeting that man today, I would never think about not wanting my child."

"Really?"

"Mmmhhhhmmm. And you want to know what else I found out? Takeya is my fucking sister. And I think her ass has known the whole time."

"Damn. Watch yo' back. It's always some snakes close by."

"Exactly." I agreed.

"I'm happy as fuck you handled yo' shit today. But take yo' clothes off. I want you naked face down ass up."

"Say less, daddy." It was time to play now.

I did just like my man said, took off my clothes fast as hell, got up on our bed and got on all fours. Then looked behind myself, bit my lip and waited to see his dick. I wasn't shy about it either. I loved looking at the mothafucka.

"This what you looking for?" He said right before sliding in my pussy.

I couldn't keep my head turned anymore. I put my face down like daddy said and tooted my ass up more. Letting him fill me up. There was nothing like that make up sex when everything in the world felt right again.

Imani

A week ago I lost mine and King's baby. A part of me felt like it died along with him. I felt that it would have been a son. Which ate at me more. I should've known I was pregnant. Then I would have done shit completely differently. For one thing, I wouldn't have been entertaining another nigga. I blamed myself for the loss of my baby and for the loss of the love Khalil used to have for me.

I had been hopeful that we could still make it work, get back together and shit could be good. For that brief moment in the mirror at the restaurant when I came to my damn senses and decided I couldn't even date other men. That all I wanted was the love of my life. That's what King was to me.

I was ready to face any and everything with him. Even being a step mom. Some shit I never wanted to be all for the sake of our family. But at this point it seemed like we didn't have a path forward together. I was struggling worse than I'd ever struggled just to get out of damn bed each morning and find a reason to live. It wasn't over a nigga. It was over EVERYTHING. Life just never get easier.

On top of all the shit that I was battling mentally, this nigga Marcus had sent me that video. Followed up with trying to black mail me. I didn't know what the hell I was going to do. He wanted a quarter million to keep quiet and not send the video to King. I knew we weren't together, but there was no way I could let Khalil see the shit in that video.

It was something I couldn't even bare to watch myself. I just wanted the whole thing to go away and be forgotten about. No woman should have to watch themselves being violated. The worst part was you couldn't tell that I was out of it from the camera angle. A regular ass person would think the whole thing was consensual.

Reluctantly, I sat up and scrolled through my phone. Then forced myself to get up out of bed. About 15 minutes later I was getting another message from this nigga like clockwork. Demanding I western union him the money "or else". The shit was getting old as hell. It had been so bad lately that the stress led me to bite off my acrylic nails. Now a bitch was left biting the real ones down to damn nubs. My nails never looked this bad. On top of that, I took my braids out myself after coming home from the hospital. I didn't want any part of me to be like it was the night that I was desperately trying to forget.

Now when I looked in the mirror I hardly recognized myself. The bruises on my cheeks, legs, ass and stomach were healed. The bleeding from the miscarriage had stopped. But that didn't stop the real hurt. Nothing did.

I didn't respond right away to this sick nigga's messages. Instead I got in the shower. Deciding to go in to school for the day. I had 3 weeks left until I graduated. That shit was all I had going for me right now. That damn degree was the carrot I needed. After getting out of my quick shower, I threw on my fit for school. Lotioning up my body first. Then I put grey leggings on with an oversized off the shoulder black sweat shirt with PINK written across the front. My look matched my feelings but like it or not I still had it going on which I wasn't trying to do. I smoothed back my hair and edges. Keeping my natural hair tied back in a low ponytail.

I woke Amyra up and got her ready. She was grumpy and wanted to keep sleeping. I had to smile at her bad ass attitutde just like her Aunt B, I swear they were twins with this sleeping shit.

I dropped her off then went to the college. Since I was early for my first class, I sat in the car and started looking at Western Union online. It was a lot of fucking money, but I had more than $250,000 in my savings. King's deposits had increased with his success in the streets. I hated taking money from him, so he did the shit without me knowing most of the time and I ignored it. The deposit went through last week like normal, even on bad terms.

A quarter mill was still a big ass chunk of change. That shit was going to set me back on my dream of owning my restaurant. Khalil did the most when it came to my goals. He was my biggest support. I knew I'd never find another man like him. Not for me. The love we had was one of a kind.

A single tear fell from my eye. I wiped it away. I was tired of being weak and sad all the damn time. Western Union only allowed $2500 a day to be transferred. The more I thought on it, the more I realized that this nigga who was trying to blackmail me had to be stupid as hell. Why would he risk staying around and in contact with me? He had to know who King was for him to be attempting to get so much money. I could use that shit against him.

Fuck it, it was time for me to step up and take care of my damn self and handle my own shit. Without counting on any nigga to come rescue me. Especially when I had been let down more times than I could count. I liked to think of myself as independent, a go getter and all this positive shit. And for the most part I was all of those things. But when it came to men, I had been weak and passive. Pathetic. Well not anymore. I wasn't living in fear or self pity another damn day. And I didn't want my daughter to grow up and be weak either. I needed to do this shit for myself and for her.

So I sent this nigga a message, telling him about the transfer limit and telling him I'd leave a bag with cash for him in a public place. That I'd send him the address later and I wanted an exchange with the video and any and all copies with it in another duffle bag at the time of the meet up.

I knew he'd probably still have copies of the shit. But that wasn't my reason for any of this. I wanted to face him in person and let him know he didn't have any power over me. Plus I had a plan. Marcus wasn't getting away with any of the shit he did to me, just to do it to another women next time. This shit was coming to an end and I was going to be the one to stop it.

I hit up my bestie and asked her to meet up for lunch after class. She had a morning one too, so it was perfect. During my class, the instructor went over the guidelines for our final submissions. That would count for half our grades. I only paid half attention, jotting down the notes I needed but my mind was consumed with planning the shit out for later.

By the time both my morning classes were over, I was hungry. Having a real ass appetite for the first time all week. This plan better work. At lunch I ran shit down to Brandi. And she told me all about how our other "bestie" had always been on straight bullshit. Takeya was fraud as hell. And even though I was focused today on the shit with ol' boy Marcus, we weren't going to let that snake ass shit she pulled slide either. People were going to learn not to fuck with us.

Rosaria

Just like a good faithful dog, King came back like I knew he would. All my plans were working. One thing about me is that I never was a bitch to sit back and lose. I was a born winner. I don't know what King and his little temporary replacement thought. Especially King. He had been with me for years and should've known I wasn't the bitch to play with.

All I had to do was put in a couple of phone calls. And that was all she wrote. Now things were coming together. King was laying in my bed like I wanted too. I took the opportunity to get a picture of his ass sleeping. And posted it to snap, Instagram and Facebook with the caption, "baby daddy" adding heart emojis. Yes, I was petty but I wanted to make sure word got back to his old hoe. She needed to know that I wasn't going any fucking where. I was here to stay, and her time was up.

Everything was basically secured, my position locked in. All that was left were the final touches to secure the bag and my nigga. This bitch might have been pretty, but that was it. She was stupid as hell and way out of her league dealing with a nigga like King in the first place. She never even saw the threat coming with how weak she was. I laughed to myself. It couldn't have been me.

My phone rang in my hand right after I finished commenting on the picture I just posted when one of my social media friends commented. I thought my shit was on silent. And when I looked at the screen and saw it was Marcus calling, I rushed to get up out of the bed, practically jumping up.

"What?" I whispered into the phone with a bad ass attitude.

"Damn, what's yo' problem?"

"Nigga, shut up!" I pressed the bathroom door closed and looked at myself in the bathroom mirror.

Holding the phone with my shoulder and chin, so I could free up my hands. Fixing my hair, waiting to hear why the hell I was getting this call first thing in the morning. He knew better than to call at any time, unless it was important. So this shit better be worth the risk of King finding out. Because when it came down to it, I knew how that nigga got down in the streets. And when he felt betrayed he was ruthless. I had seen a small part of that side of him and didn't want to test his gangster further.

"Aight, fine. I see how you're acting. Don't let that shit go to your fucking head. 'Cus that nigga might be onto us."

"What you mean?"

"I thought you'd want to know the nigga you claiming yo' baby father just got rid of the real one."

"Are you serious?"

"Oh, now you want to listen. Well don't say I didn't warn you. It's some shit coming yo' way. You need to get the fuck on. Lay low until it blows over."

"I can't do that. That'll make shit worse. King doesn't suspect me, but he will if I switch up. This all just might work in our favor, Let me feel things out first."

"Aight. But be careful. I got shit moving on my end. Get up with me if anything changes. Otherwise we'll stick to the plan."

"Okay. And don't call again. I'll call you if I need to. It's too risky now that I'm back with King."

I heard footsteps in the bedroom and quickly hung the damn phone up. Nervous as hell that King might've been up and heard some shit that I said. Even though I had turned the water on, so it ran in the background and I stayed whispering. My heart was beating fast and I unintentionally stuck my fingers in mouth. Biting my nails without thinking. I caught myself though. If King saw that shit, he'd know I was lying about something. He knew my habits like that from when we were a real ass couple. He always paid attention to details like no other nigga I'd ever met. It wasn't out of his love. Even though he did love my ass at one point and would do almost damn near anything for me. He was just like that with everything and everyone. Which is why I couldn't switch up a single fucking thing I did with my actions or habits. That shit would send a warning to him and he would for sure figure out there was a connection between me and Demont at least. Even if not with the other shit that was happening afoot right now. I don't know if he would kill me, but I wasn't taking the chance. The baby wouldn't keep me safe. That shit I did know.

All I could do now was stick to the plan. Play it cool and hopefully my role would be enough to put King at ease. At least now there wasn't another nigga alive that could claim my daughter outside of King.

Imani

Me and Brandi were headed to the meet up spot. I swear to God my skin was already crawling with apprehension thinking about this low down dirty ass nigga. The shit made me sick to my stomach and I wasn't even face to face with him yet. But I knew I needed to face him. Face this shit and get out of that victim mentality. I never wanted to be that type of woman.

Brandi was driving separate in her own car. The plan was for me to get the video by him handing over his phone while I gave his ass a bag full of money. I didn't give a fuck about the money because this was just the beginning of what I had planned for his ass. He wasn't about to get away with a damn thing. Bet that shit.

I pulled up to the shopping center lot, which was an outdoor mall type place. On the nicer side of town. We were supposed to meet out in front of the bookstore where there was a courtyard with benches and tables. That way I thought it would look the least suspicious.

I was about 15 minutes early on purpose. I texted Brandi who I saw pulling into the entrance down one from where I came in at. She played shit cool and parked adjacent to where I was headed to sit down and wait. I got out of my ride and walked over, with the bag swung across my chest. Looking like a simple black gym bag. Nobody should expect that there was stacks of paper, it wasn't all of what Marcus asked for. But it was the most I could withdraw in one transaction today with short notice. So it was what it was. His ass didn't need to know the details anyway and if I read his ass right he wasn't going to say shit on it. He would be happy thinking he got over on my ass again. Like he had power and control over me. But that was only in his damn mind, nothing else.

I sat waiting. It seemed like longer than it was. I kept my phone in my hand, scrolling through Instagram like I normally would if I was sitting out here waiting for regular shit. But damn sure checking the time steadily keeping track. Sure enough, this nigga walked up right on time. I didn't stare but I watched unenthusiastically. The look I gave him on our fake ass date was nothing like the one I shot him now.

I couldn't even help the natural frown I felt myself giving him if I wanted to. This nigga disgusted me. But instead of the fear I thought I would feel, when he got close all I felt was the power he thought he took from me. And he didn't even know what I had in store for his ass. Last time he had me at his mercy, drugged and out of it. He really was the weak one in this shit. And soon enough he'd find that out first hand.

That stupid ass smirk on his face said it all. When he spoke, I wanted to throw up right on his corny fake ass.

"What's good sexy. You miss me?"

"You got the phone?"

I stood up and took a step in the opposite direction of him, keeping space between us. He reached in his jeans pocket and pulled it out. Then held out his hand.

"Here."

"Unlock the shit first nigga."

He chuckled. Pissing me off more. But I kept my cool. The longer I stood here, the more I wanted to swing on this nigga and go in on his ass. I was shaking that's how I was feeling. This nigga was foul as hell and it took every fiber of my being to keep my composure. I silently reminded myself of the "bigger picture" and counted to 5 in my head, taking steady breaths and making sure my eyes averted his. Watching his hands and phone. Until he held the shit out again and I took it. Going right to the gallery, where I saw the videos. Yes, this nigga had more than one. I went into settings, changed the password and screen saver. Then held it in the grip of my left hand. Gestured my other hand towards the bag that I left sitting on the bench.

Before walking the fuck away. Without looking back. Going straight to my car. When I got inside I let the frustration get the best of me. I hit the steering wheel repeatedly, still shaking now more than ever. And a few tears escaped my eyes. Not sad shit, angry ones. I was a woman scorned, and mad as hell. This nigga was going to pay for everything. I put that shit on my daughter. I calmed my breathing down. Then looked in the mirror, fixing my face.

A few minutes later and the text I was waiting for came through from Brandi. Yes, my bitch was on his ass now. See he thought I was just letting shit slide. That I was fool enough to take the phone and let him be. Brandi was sitting, waiting for him to leave so she could follow his ass. Find out where he laid his head. Then we were going to pay his nasty ass a visit. He liked to rape women, well we were going to have a little fun with him tonight. Like I said. The weak version of myself was gone. Now I was out for vengeance and blood.

Khalil (King)

"What the fuck was you doing in there?" I said as soon as Rosaria came out the bathroom.

I knew I shouldn't have stayed over, but I was tired as hell. I didn't even fuck. As bad as this bitch tried, I couldn't even keep a hard dick with her ass anymore. I couldn't trust her and with that any and everything was gone. The one time since breaking up with Imani was because I was drunk as hell and it was on some aggressive shit. The same type of shit that got me into this situation with being a soon to be father.

But I was really done with her ass. No part of me wanted her. She wasn't for me. It was simple as hell. When I woke up in her bed, I felt that shit was a done fucking deal. I didn't do regrets and shit but I knew I shouldn't be here. Shit was off. And my gut was telling me this bitch was up to some grimy shit.

So when I heard her voice all quiet in the bathroom talking to some mothafucka, I knew I was right. My instincts were never off. When I felt it, it was real. Rosaria was an enemy. If I learned anything from being around her those years, it was that she was behind the shit with Imani somehow too. Or at least knew something about it.

I needed to keep her real close and find out the extent of the bullshit she was pulling. It also made me doubt more than I already did that the seed she was carrying was mine. A grimy ass bitch like her couldn't be trusted about a gotdamn thing.

That DNA test was coming the minute the baby was out of her pussy.

After I called her ass out, this bitch caught a fucking attitude when she came out of the bathroom. I wasn't going for it, already putting my fucking shoes on and tucking my tool in the back of my pants.

"Where you going daddy? It better not be to see that bitch."

"Watch yo' fucking mouth."

I wasn't trying to get in a fucking argument, but Rosaria was determined to be on some bullshit for real. Her ass didn't know I was onto her and didn't give a fuck.

"I'm telling you right now King, you better not have her around our child. I don't play that. You might like to play step daddy but I don't want no bitch playing step mom. Play with me if you want to. I only tolerate the shit you got going on because I fucked up. But I'm hoping in time you can forgive me. I love you. And I want us to be a family. A real family. Our child deserves for us to at least try."

I almost laughed out loud, but played shit cool. Keeping my face like fucking steal and not showing any sign of how wrong she had shit figured in her fucked up bird brain. A nigga like me never forgave betrayal. Not when our heart was on the fucking line. If a street nigga gave you his heart the worst thing you could do was turn your back when he was behind them bars. The second worst thing was give his pussy away. She did both at the same time. That was a wrap for me. I wasn't a clown ass nigga that would ever let a bitch waiver when it came to loyalty.

I was a King out here. Building my shit from the ground up. Me and my niggas were the mothafuckas running shit. I wasn't settling when it came to the bitch I settled down with. The woman I chose had to be a reflection of me in every way.

Imani came to mind, and that shit hurt. I stood up, walked towards the bedroom door. But I guess Rosaria wasn't trying to accept me not giving her a fucking answer. She stepped in front of the doorway, so I couldn't get the fuck out.

"You need to give me an answer!" She demanded.

"Move out the fucking way. I ain't got time for this shit."

"You better make time."

"Get the fuck on, before I make yo' ass. Damn."

"Nigga, I wish you would put yo' hands on me." She folded her arms right under her titties on top of her big ass stomach.

Too much fucking drama and attitude for no fucking reason. I didn't beat on women at all. Lovely brought me up right. She would've beat my ass if I tried it. Nah, that was some sucka ass shit. But I wasn't above touching her ass. She was doing too fucking much. I grabbed her by the sides and picked her small ass up. Rosaria wasn't nothing but 5 foot 2 and all titties, ass and now stomach. I set her down to the side and got the fuck on.

I had to stay the fuck from her ass for a minute, just play my role nothing more or less. Find out what the fuck she was up to by keeping close enough. Since she was being stupid as hell. I had too much shit to lose and so did my fucking team behind the dumb shit.

I drove over to my new place, on the way South headed to the arcade. Close by I saw a barbershop I'd never been to and decided to get a quick line up.

When I walked in the mothafucka there was only one other customer and one barber working. So I went to sit down on a chair to wait my turn to get my shit cut. There was this bad ass bitch standing to the side of one of the empty chairs, turned around talking on the phone. I couldn't help notice all that ass behind her since she was turned around. It was only right to look. But when she turned around and smiled I was caught staring for real. She was beautiful as hell, stacked, straight white teeth, and real ass hair to her shoulders. She was put together and bad. I figured she must be the nigga cutting hair's bitch because there was no other reason for her to be sitting up in a barber shop.

"Can I help you?" She asked from across the shop.

"I'm just waiting my turn for a chair."

Shorty bit her bottom lip, eyed me up and down. Released her lip from between her teeth and got closer to the chair.

"I got you."

"You cut hair?" I stood up.

Fuck it, I was letting her even if she didn't.

"Yes, I cut hair. I wouldn't say I got you if I didn't, now would I?"

I liked her attitude too. She could fucking talk. A lot of these bitches couldn't put a sentence together for real. It was just something about her. And when I caught her ass looking down at my dick print in the grey sweats I was wearing, I knew she was feeling a nigga back.

About 15 minutes later, after silence and a fresh line up I was done. I got back up handed her a hundred. Told her to keep the change and asked for her number. She told me her name was Ma'Lena and ran off her numbers. When she asked for my number I was surprised but I actually gave her my shit. Well the number to my work line. That way if this bitch was crazy I wouldn't have to change my regular one. Plus I wasn't looking for nothing serious. But something down here wasn't a bad idea since I was back and forth so much.

I headed out of the shop and finished my day in the arcade, before making my way back North to Wilmington. Another shipment was coming in tomorrow and I had to get the niggas on board with the movements bright and early. Keeping everything to the last minute so that if there was a rat in our camp, there'd be less time for them to impact our shit. The last thing we needed was a confiscation or some other fuck up.

It was going to be a late ass night. But staying busy kept me focused and my mind off of my personal shit.

Imani

Brandi called me within thirty minutes with an address. She had followed that nigga Marcus and now had an address for where he was staying. In order to not lose eyes on him, we decided that I would drive to where she was. And we'd wait outside until nightfall. He was too sure of himself to even be looking for my car even if he paid attention to the shit I drove.

I pulled into the parking lot of a hotel following the directions in my phone that Brandi sent. She told me it was a hotel but this nigga wasn't staying at the same type of shit he raped me at. Nope. Now that this mothafucka thought he was balling, he was in a nicer hotel. Still away from Downtown near the North side of the city altogether. Out of the way, but still close enough. He was damn sure up to some other shit it seemed like. I still didn't understand why he targeted me. Khalil warned me about enemies and shit. People who would use me to get at him. I had been naïve to that side of our life. And it had cost me our child.

I didn't want to think about that right now though. I needed to feel my anger towards this nigga. He wasn't getting away with hurting my family. I was handling his ass, getting my money back and then going back home to focus on being a better mother and person all around. This shit damn near broke me, but I was determined to fight through all the pain and come out on top.

Hurrying up, I hopped out of my car after turning it off. Hit the key fob and locked my doors, then walked over the two rows getting closer to the building where Brandi was parked. She was sitting up staring straight ahead serious as hell when I got in next to her.

"Bitch. It's 'bout time you get here. I need some company. This shit got me paranoid as a mothafucka."

"Sis, I really appreciate you doing this for me."

"Stop right there. You already know how we get down. If they fuck with one, they fuckin' with both. Right!?"

"You know it!" I cosigned.

Having her with me in this shit lifted the burden off of me. At the same time having to admit my fuck up and where I went wrong trusting this nigga even for a damn second was some hard shit to do. My pride made it hard for me to look in the mirror and swallow that pill. I should've known better no matter how much she reassured me. I knew deep down I should've never let this man get the best of me.

"There he go!" Brandi pointed.

And sure enough the nigga was coming out the front of the hotel. Then just stood over to the side. Luckily on the side further from where we were parked. Plus Brandi parked in the row back on the other side of the median behind some fucking bushes. Her car sat low so it was like we were in the cut. But we had a clear view of Marcus.

It didn't look like his ass wasn't doing much. Just on the phone and smoking. Looking way too comfortable to be a nigga with my money.

Just as soon as he put his phone in his pocket, his head turned to the entrance of the hotel parking lot as a car turned in. The silver Honda turned in and then parked in one of the closer spots by where he was standing. Marcus walked over to the car and then waited for whoever was behind the wheel to get out.

When the door opened, it just had to be the same bitch that I couldn't fucking escape from. Khalil's ex who was about to fucking drop his so called baby was hugging on this nigga. I went ahead and snapped a picture zooming in on my phone.

"You see this shit? These mothafuckas think they can play with my fucking life."

"What you want to do?" Brandi asked.

I didn't answer right away. Whatever exchange the two of them had going on was quick as hell. The hoe was getting back in her car just as damn fast driving back off. The nigga threw down his cigarette looked around and then walked back in the hotel.

"Let's wait a few more minutes. Then go up to his room. You play like you're a friend of that bitch he know. Since ya'll both pregnant. Then we bust in on him and make him tell us what the fuck game they got going on."

"Okay, but how will we know what room he's in?"

"Let me worry about that." I reassured, even though I didn't have an answer myself really.

We waited. Really going into the hotel was winging it. I didn't have a clue how we were going to go about things. Getting the room number or none of it. But I knew I had to make shit happen, I couldn't sit back and let this nigga win. Him and that bitch cost me everything.

I led the way, with Brandi walking steadily behind me. Went up to the front desk and played shit off.

"Excuse me, I uh forgot my room key. Can I get another one please?"

"Sure no problem ma'am. What's your room number?"

"Oh, uh. Well I can't remember. Let me think..." I paused and played shit off. Literally twiddling my damn thumbs on the counter. "I really can't remember at all. But it's under my boyfriend's name. Marcus... Dewey." I thankfully remembered the name he gave me during dinner. Before I was out of it. I hoped that was his real ass name. There was no telling what the nigga lied about.

"Here it is, Room 311."

"Thank you so much. I really appreciate it."

"Your welcome."

The card was keyed and then I took it ready to get up to the room and confront this grimy nigga.

We walked over to the elevator and then got in.

177

"Brandi, I want you to stay back. Don't even come in the room sis. I got this and if Coup even knew your ass was here or that I involved you in this shit, he'd be trying to murder mine and yo' ass for sure."

"Shit, that man can't control what I do. I'm here because I will always have your back. Point blank period. Plus this nigga isn't that stupid. If he really comes against both of us the whole East side will be on his ass. He'd be dead by the end of the week. He ain't stupid. That's why he did some low down shit behind the scenes. Knowing it wouldn't go public and niggas on our side wouldn't know the shit he did."

"Yeah, you're right. He thinks he won too."

"Mmmmhhhm."

The elevator chimed and the door opened to the third floor. I peeked out like I was on some movie or some shit. But didn't see anyone in sight either way. So I pushed the hold the door open button and then stepped off. Letting Brandi follow behind.

"I'm gonna go in and then get the cash. If you hear me yell out "CALL" That means call King and tell him what's going on. I don't think it will come anywhere near that. But just in case. I won't be more than a few minutes. Keep a lookout and knock on the door if you see that bitch coming up."

Brandi nodded in agreement, pulled out her cell phone and stayed to the side of the door against the wall. I walked right up to the door, pressed my cheek and ear against the cool wood.

Trying to listen for any sounds inside. All I could hear was the TV playing with indistinct sounds. No footsteps that I could tell. Shit I couldn't really tell at all. So I looked at Brandi, then took a deep breath and put the key in the door lock system. Saw the light turn green and slid it out. Turned the knob down as quiet as possible. Then held it still, waiting a few seconds to see if this nigga came to the door form the sound. I released the breath that I was holding in. And pushed the door open.

Hurrying up, I stepped inside. Quickly closing the shit right back behind me. Making sure to hold it steady to avoid the loud ass "CLICK" when it was closed.

I made it inside the room. And instantly heard the shower running, noticed the door closed and the light on in the bathroom. So I crept further inside from the entrance. I pulled my gun out. The 9 mm Taurus Khalil bought me this past Christmas. I was by no means an expert. But I knew how to shoot and believe me this nigga was first on my list to test that shit out. I couldn't be that scary ass female any more. It was time to boss up and handle myself, by myself. I didn't need King to come to the rescue this time. My life was in my hands.

Looking around the empty hotel room, I didn't see the duffle bag I handed off to Marcus earlier right away. So I walked over to the side of the bed closest to the window. Still nothing. Then began pulling out drawers. When I got to the second one down, I found what I was looking for.

The bag was tucked inside. I pulled it out, threw the strap over my shoulder. Still holding the gun in my right hand.

I turned around and got ready to head out of the room. Making a clean break for it without even having to confront this nigga. But that's not how shit ended up playing out. As soon as I stepped forward, the bathroom door swung open. I dodged out of the way and hid my body behind the wall. Staying close to it so Marcus couldn't see my ass right away.

He walked out, just past the wall, wearing only a towel around his waist. I wasn't interested in him at all sexually. I was disgusted. But at this point my instincts kicked in and I was all adrenalin.

"Nigga, back the fuck up!" I said loud and firm.

"What the fuck? Bitch you better drop that fucking bag." He countered eyeing the bag around my shoulder.

"Fuck you!" I shouted loud as hell.

Then fired the gun aiming for his leg. The kick from the shot jolted me out of my angry state and into reality fast as hell.

He was shot, blood started staining the white towel above his knee somewhere around his thigh. He started to lunge towards me, I aimed the gun again and shot a second time near the same as the first. Hitting flesh again. This time the impact caused him to slump over onto the bed to the side.

Bracing himself only with his arm. He screamed out in pain, "Bitch YOU SHOT ME!"

"You lucky I'm letting you live."

Then I walked past him in a damn near run, spit on him and got the fuck out of the room. I knew the police had been called already. I saw Brandi wide eyed waiting outside the room for me, holding the phone to her ear. She hurried up right along with me, grabbing my hand and pulling my ass down towards the stairway exit.

She was 9 months pregnant, running and shit like she wasn't carrying my niece. I felt bad for dragging her into my mess. Especially with how shit went down. I didn't mean for shit to go this far. I heard sirens in the background getting closer. By the time we made it to the first floor, we caught a glimpse of them entering back through the main entrance lobby all the way down the hall from where the back exit we were leaving from was. I quickly turned my head, slowed us both down. And we walked out as calm as possible. I didn't notice that the gun was still in my hand so I tucked it into the front of my pants. As awkward as that was it was better than being identified as the damn shooter. We got in each of our cars and drove out the exit while the 3 police cars were pulled right up to the front entrance.

I knew I had fucked up. I knew that there was most likely security cameras. My emotions had gotten the best of me. I panicked. I should have never even came here. Regret filled me while I drove to my house. Brandi sent me a text that said she was going home and that I needed to go home too.

I knew she was right. I didn't know what my next move would be. But I felt like there was going to be some serious fall out for the shit I just pulled. As much regret as I felt. I also felt a sense of power and relief. I finally took charge and bossed up. No nigga was ever going to push me around again or get the best of me. All the shit that I'd been through had changed me. And it wasn't like I killed the man.

Khalil (King)

Getting that phone call from Brandi set me off. That shit had me in my whip and on my way to the fucking hotel Imani was at with that fuck nigga, 40 out on my lap ready to run up in that bitch and take all the risks. Ready to go to fucking war without a second thought. By the time I crossed the bridge, Brandi hit me back and told me they left the spot.

She let me know that Imani was headed home. All I could say back into the phone to her was "good". Then I hung up. And hit Coup up.

"Bruh, check yo' ol' lady. She and Imani running 'round on bullshit. I'm headed to deal with mine now."

"Say less. She supposed to know better couzo."

We hung up and then I lit up the rest of my blunt from earlier. If I didn't smoke before I faced Imani I knew there would be no telling what the fuck what would happen. From what little bit that Brandi told me over the phone they followed the bitch ass nigga back to his hotel. Then came up with the fucking brilliant idea to run up on him. Two bitches. One about to drop my niece any day and one who just lost her baby a few weeks ago. I don't know what the fuck they were on or thinking. Imani lost her damn mind.

I got to the house before Imani did. So I pulled around the block and walked around up the walkway. Then used my old key to go inside. Letting

183

myself in and keeping all the lights off. To surprise Imani.

She came in, not even paying attention that the door and security system were already off. It was shit like this that pissed me off. She didn't fucking pay attention. She really had no fucking clue how reckless she moved out here. I thought she would get the fucking message with all the bullshit that had happened to her but obviously not.

"What the fuck are you doing shorty?"

"Wha-a-a...?"

"Man, you got to do better than this. On some real shit, what the fuck were you thinking?" I stood up, walked over to her and backed her up into the kitchen island.

My voice got loud and I wasn't even a loud type nigga. My blood was boiling. She was doing the stupidest shit and risking everything. Her life, Amyra's, and everything we had built so far. I couldn't understand why she didn't understand basic ass shit. But I was about to make her understand. Shit couldn't continue like this.

"You know what KING! Just get the fuck out! Okay? I mean why are you even here? Why are YOU worried about what I do or don't do?"

She turned some, put her purse down and then faced me head on. Folded her arms. With some shit I'd never seen in her eyes before. It was anger and strength. The old Imani would have cowered away, cried or some shit to get through whatever she was dealing with. And I loved that shit

184

about her. She was real and that shit was hard to find in a woman.

But I couldn't even front, this side to her. Bossing up and standing her ground against me made me want to fuck her up and bend her ass over at the same time.

"I'm not going nowhere! You understand? This shit between us ain't never stopping. I'm always gon' be here for you regardless. You should know that shit baby."

"Mmmhhhmmm. Whatever nigga. That's what you say but where were you when that nigga was raping me? Where were you when I lost our child? So you know what... save all your talking for a bitch who believes it. I'm not the one anymore. I handled shit. End of story. You walked away when I was at my lowest. Don't you get it?"

Imani's eyes got watery. But she held back tears. I didn't realize I had fucked up on my end so bad. The shit was hurting her worse than I even knew.

"You not gon' disrespect me. I don't give a fuck what we been through or going through. That shit's never gon' fly. You don't have to do this shit alone. I'm here. I'm so fucking sorry yo. I been fucking up. But I'm nothing without you. I'm gon' make all this shit right. On God. I told you day 1, I got you. That shit hasn't changed. I still got you."

I reached up on either side of her head, and pulled her head against mine firmly. Her forehead touching my lips. I began laying kisses all over her skin.

185

Instead of pulling back she let me touch her and kiss on her. I moved my hands, to her titties sitting up right under her shirt. Pulled back and tongue kissed her. Deep as fuck, sucking on her bottom lip, then biting it before moving to her neck. I took my time with every part of her body. Trying to take away her anger and erase the bad memories of us falling out. Right now there was none of that. Just my love and my dick. And this mothafucka missed his home.

I pulled off her pants. While she lifted her shirt up over her head. Picked her up, cupping her fat ass in the palms of my hands. Imani wrapped her legs around me. And I walked her down the hall towards the bedroom. Her panties and bra the only thing on her perfect light brown skin. The house was dark, but there was a light on in the bathroom at the end of the hall that led the way.

We stayed locked, kissing until I got her to the room and threw her down on the bed. She took off her bra and I went and pulled her white see through shit down. Took off my shirt and pants. Then got on the bed with her, turned her to the side and got to work eating her pussy. She tasted good as fuck. Like candy and water. I sucked and licked. Latched onto her clit and vibrated my throat. Flicking my tongue in and out of her pussy. Found her clit and sucked hard. Imani's hands held tight as hell onto my head. Her nails rubbing against my waves holding my face in place. She was the only bitch I was tasting. She was mine and we both knew that shit. No matter what the circumstance this is where we would end up.

Her hand found my dick and she started stroking the big mothafucka up and down, gripping it to the rhythm I was eating her.

"Fuck! What are you doing to me?"

I didn't stop or say shit. Just kept sucking and enjoying all her juices in my mouth. Her legs locked around me and her grip on my dick locked in place. As her body tensed up she screamed out and then her body shook as her water came rushing out. I kept sucking and let her ride that shit out.

Then roughly spread her legs wider, got between them and lifted them up. Slid my dick in. Feeling her walls clamp down on my shit. I gripped her ass and pulled her towards me. Until my dick was as deep as it would go.

"AHHHHHH! Shit."

"I don't want to hear that shit. Take yo' dick shorty."

"I'm 'bout to cum again bae." Imani moaned.

She threw her head back, but I wanted to watch the look on her face and look into her eyes. Sometimes we made love, other times we fucked. Tonight we were fucking. And the way her pussy was feeling, I wasn't even gonna last as long as usual.

"Stop fucking moving and watch. Take the mothafucka." I bit my bottom lip.

Imani tilted her chin down and did like I told her. Watching my dick slide in and out of her pussy. Then I pulled her legs up, held onto her knees and started going harder in and out at an angle.

"AHHHHH, SSSSS, AHHHH!" Her loud ass moans filled the room.

She started wiggling and shit sliding around underneath me. I knew I was hitting her spot and she couldn't take the shit and that's what had her doing all that extra shit.

"Stop fucking moving."

"I can't. OH MY GOD!"

Her body tensed up again and she froze. Her body shaking all over even from her breathing. Her expression looking strained, to her pussy squeezing my dick. Tightening up all over. I bent down and started sucking on her hard ass nipples. Paying attention to each one. Letting my hands roam all over her. I pulled her up by the shoulders and had her bent up like a fucking pretzel.

"Let that shit out." I told her.

And just like that on cue. My words and the way our bodies was joined, set off the climax her body was wanting. Imani screamed out. Clawed my back with her nails. And then fell back against the bed.

She wasn't getting off that easy. I wasn't done. I laid kisses on her body, neck and then we started kissing that intense deep shit. The only bitch who could make my body respond like this was her and she better know that shit.

Once she recovered I flipped her over and spread her just enough to slide my dick inside from

188

the back. Gripped her by the waist and scooted her down on the bed closer to me so she couldn't run from the dick. I wanted to reach her fucking stomach and feel every part of her.

I slapped her ass. Watched the shit shake. Then slapped her other ass cheek. Held onto the fat mothafucka and tore that pussy up. Imani pressed her face down into the pillows, moaning. And tooted that ass up for me.

"Like that bae?"

"You better start calling me daddy."

"Who?" She turned around.

Looked over her shoulder. Arched her back more. And tried to open her legs to get up on her knees.

"Lay the fuck down."

I slapped her ass hard as hell again. Pushed her back down. Closed her legs back for her. Then moved one of my hands over her head. Held her hands together against the mattress so she really couldn't go no fucking where. And used my other hand to leverage my body up. Straight diving in that pussy from above.

"Say that shit."

Still nothing. Imani was hard headed. But she was gonna take the dick just like this. And I was hearing her call me daddy. Bet that shit.

I let her hands go. Then gripped her hair instead. Slowed up my pace, but made sure to lay the pipe right. Touching all of her walls and rotating around each time I was deep inside. To the base.

Then whispered in her ear low.

"What's my name?" Then yanked her by the hair and went back to fucking her hard. A few pumps in and out.

"YES DADDY!!! SHIT, FUCK!!!"

My dick started jumping at the same time as her pussy gripped my shit and ass even clenched under me. I kissed and bit down on the back of her neck. Let go of her hair and buried my dick deep inside of her while I busted. Letting all my seeds off inside her. Hoping I got her ass pregnant again. I was daddy and she was momma. This shit was a wrap.

We took our time washing each other in the shower. I made sure to be gentle when I took the washcloth and lathered it up with her vanilla shit to wash her pussy. Knowing Imani was sore from the beating it just took. By the time she started washing my body and got down to my dick. I already wanted some more pussy. We spent another 30 minutes in the shower sucking and fucking, washing each other again until the water ran cold. I couldn't get enough of this woman. Being around her now, I was remembering how good that shit felt. Just to be in her presence. She was the only bitch who made me feel something.

After the fucking and love making, we laid in bed naked under the covers. Not having to go pick up Amyra until tomorrow from her grandma's house.

"Tell me what happened?"

"I don't want to talk about that night. I don't ever want to."

"I'll respect you on that for now. But you gon' have to eventually. Otherwise that shit won't ever go away. It'll stay with you." I kissed her shoulder.

We laid with our bodies completely wrapped up in each others. Imani's leg between mine, her hand on my dick the way I liked. Holding the mothafucka. With my arms wrapped all around her shoulder and neck. She was up under me. The way it was supposed to be.

"Go 'head and tell me 'bout today."

"I met up with the nigga and handed over $150,000 from my account. Since he was trying to extort me and had a video of the shit he did to me that night. We planned it so Brandi was parked in her car and she followed him to see where he was staying. When she saw it was a hotel, she hit me up and I met her there. It was my idea to go in and confront him. I planned on getting my money back and he already had handed over the phone with the video. Well one thing led to another and when I was leaving he came out of the bathroom. I shot him in the leg twice."

Imani shrugged her shoulders under me. She didn't sound scared or like she regretted the shit.

"They got cameras at hotels shorty."

"I know, I know! But at the time I wasn't thinking 'bout that to be honest. I was mad as hell and my instincts took over. I don't regret none of the shit. Except having Brandi there. She shouldn't

191

have come in with me, because shit could've gone bad for her. Otherwise, I wish I had on a disguise or some shit. But I am glad I shot the man. He had that coming plus more. He's lucky I aimed for his leg. Because the way I was feeling, I wanted to kill his ass."

I nodded behind her. I understood and I couldn't say shit about her getting her revenge. But now my mind was thinking about how the fuck to get her out of this shit. At least there wasn't a body behind her moves. But this nigga was definitely a dead mothafucka. And if Imani still wanted, she could be there when the time came. But with me being in the streets we wanted to keep 12 off our backs on all fronts. She was tied to me plain and simple. Plus she could be charged behind this shit. Which was likely since it was at a hotel and shit. Fuck it, I was calling the lawyer we had recently paid to stay on retainer for bullshit like this. I thought it'd be for me or the niggas. Not Imani.

"I'll take care of it. It's gon' be some shit behind this. But we got a good ass lawyer if it comes to that. And I'm gon' find this nigga hopefully before it gets to that."

"When you find him, I want to be there. I know you have kept that part of your life away from me and Amyra. And you don't want me involved. And believe me, I really don't want to be. My dream is still the same. Not to be a street King's down ass bitch. But the way all this shit keeps coming at you and ME, I feel like I need to be involved in certain shit. I can hold my own. And I can hold you down.

I'll do whatever it takes to protect our family. I want you to know that. You can count on me. I'm not a liability."

I heard what she said and respected the shit to an extent. But I wasn't trying to have her in the streets with me either. She had dreams and goals before me that I didn't want to jeopardize more than I already was. Hell, I didn't even plan on staying in the game forever myself. Shit was short term, not long term.

"I hear you." That was all I had to say for now on the subject.

Right now all I wanted to do was sleep with my bitch. In our bed and relax for the first time a long ass time. This is where I needed to be. So Imani better not try to back out again. There wasn't about to be a next time.

Brandi

I was sitting in the living room. The most uncomfortable a bitch had ever been, getting a damn earful from Coup. He had spent a straight 20 minutes talking shit. Got in my face and all. Then decided he'd stay in the damn kitchen and talk shit across the house all the way to where I was sitting. He wouldn't let the shit go.

By this point his words were being tuned out and I was done apologizing.

"Are you even fucking listening B? Do you hear me talking to you?"

"Mmmhhmm." I answered.

Sitting up against the armrest of the couch, propping my head on my hand. Keeping my elbow rested. I could fall asleep sitting up like this, with Coup going in on my ass if it wasn't for the pressure I felt all the time all over my body. This baby had really just started causing pain. My daughter's official due date was for 7 more weeks. But I was ready! I couldn't even take regular ass breaths anymore. Like I said it was always so much damn pressure.

"Brandi, I'm dead ass. Yo' ass gotta think different. You have to move different. You're somebody's mother now. What the fuck would've happened if that nigga came at ya'll?"

"Look I understand. I really do. I agree I should've called you first. But just like you, I'm gonna ride for my friend. I am sorry for worrying you."

He shook his head. Ready to talk more shit. I swear I'd never heard this much from Coup on any subject. Don't get me wrong he was outgoing and talked. But when it came to arguments and things with us. If it wasn't good shit, he didn't want to hear it or discuss it. I mean he went so far as leaving my ass alone for not agreeing with him on having a baby. That was one thing about him I appreciated. He didn't like to argue or have any kind of bullshit between us. And he hadn't been on any bullshit our entire relationship so far. Even with that whole situation with the hoe showing up here. He handled himself and the situation like a real man was supposed to. But this here, he was tripping out. And I was over it. Especially with how my mind and body was feeling.

"I'm telling you right now..."

"AHHHH!"

"What!? What's wrong?" Coup stopped his words midsentence and rushed over to where I was and put his hand on my shoulder.

"I think the baby's coming." I clenched my teeth.

This time holding in the pain I felt as my stomach tightened up. I didn't know how the hell this was supposed to feel since this was my first child. But from what Imani told me and I remember from my mother's pregnancies this was it. And I started freaking the fuck out.

"It's too soon! Coup we got to go! NOW!"

"Aight. I'm gon' get yo' shit and help you in the car. Wait right here."

195

I went to stand up. Holding my stomach with one of my hands. And put my other one on my lower back. I wasn't that big but these new contractions were some other shit. Ready or not my daughter was coming. I knew it was time to meet her and as scared as I was, my heart felt at ease. I knew it was early, so I just prayed as hard as I could that her body was ready to meet the world.

Khalil (King)

With all the bullshit of the day, business was still business. And first thing in the morning when I woke up back at my old house with Imani I knew she wasn't going to be happy with me dipping out on her so early.

I got up without disturbing her and got ready. With her little ass snores making me chuckle. Because she swore up and down she didn't snore. But I noticed every time I dicked her down and she passed out, was when she slept heavy as hell with a quiet snore. But still snored. I missed shit like that and she didn't even know it. But having my woman back had a nigga on top of the world. For that in itself, it was already a good ass day.

But I needed to run out to the arcade right now because we had our biggest shipment coming in first thing this morning. It should be arriving around 8 am. The truck stayed on the road at the least likely time to get stopped which was overnight and just before dawn. But even if they did get stopped for some bullshit violation everything looked legit. The connect hired some white mothafucka to drive who had worked with their family in other states. And the product was combined with the candy, paper and other shit so all of it stayed under the fucking radar. This time we had 2 trucks coming in. I was moving weight for some niggas in South Carolina. Becoming the new connect in town for them. But I hadn't even met them in person. Shit was done through a third

197

party. With one of our lieutenant's cousins. There were no names or faces associated with me or Coup. That was the only way I agreed to doing the shit. And as cool as Sergio was, I knew at the end of the day our relationship was superficial.

Meaning as long as the bread added up with no losses, shit was sweet. But this was big boy shit. Cartel business was the real fucking deal. And these mothafucking Columbians might not have a big ass presence here yet, but their reach was the furthest of all the drug bosses in the gotdamn world. Because they controlled the majority of the purest and most uncut shit. Point blank period. What they said went.

But when I pulled into the back lot of my arcade, behind the building where the truck should have already been, my instincts told me some shit was off. Coup wasn't here and his ass was always on time for shipments. Now with every other fucking thing the nigga slept in and kept hours like his ass still hustled the block all night. Then slept until noon.

I hit his line and the shit went straight to voicemail. I didn't know what the fuck was up. The other niggas who were supposed to help unload and unpack the shipment pulled in a few minutes after me. One of them was the same lieutenant who was responsible for breaking down and handling the new deal with the niggas down this way. I liked to see he was taking this promotion serious and got here on fucking time. One of the other lieutenants was with him. Our most loyal and trusted worker.

The nigga closest to us, right up under us next in line. The nigga we called Bruce Lee.

And the funniest shit was this nigga was the darkest skin mothafucka on the whole fucking East side you might as well say. He didn't have an ounce of fucking Asian or any type of shit like that in him. He was tall and nothing that you would think about when the nickname Bruce Lee was mentioned. He got that shit because when he was a kid out in the hood there were these two brothers who tried to jump his ass. One the same age and the other a few years older. And out of fucking nowhere, this nigga started beating both their asses. Stomping the older one out, make it so bad. Some of the old heads and shit who saw what went down began calling him Bruce Lee after that. That's just how shit stuck with you when it came to nicknames. Now that's all anyone knew his ass by. And best believe the nigga could still fight. He never lost. He didn't need to jump to shooting like a lot of these so called tough niggas around the way. And all that gun shit got exposed on inside anyway. The real and fake always separated one way or the other.

My burner phone started ringing from the center console under the armrest. I lifted the black leather top up and reached inside to pull it out. Already knowing it wasn't any good fucking news. My instincts where right on fucking target too. Sergio was on the line when I picked up.

"I need answers hombre. I haven't heard from mí hermano or my driver since yesterday. They were supposed to call me first thing en la mañana."

"Same fucking thing I need partna. I'm here now, and no trucks."

"What do you mean?"

"You tell me. It's your men in transport. All my niggas do is wait 'til the shit gets here."

"No me jodas! Don't fuck me over!" Sergio yelled into the phone. "There's a lot of money in those trucks. You need to find them. And soon! Call me back by the end of the day. And it better be with good fucking news."

He hung up in my ear. The shit he was spitting was straight bullshit. Me and my team were never responsible for the security or transport of the product. That was never in our agreement. When I first took on Sergio as a plug he knew that I was fresh out and a small time hustler trying to break into some real pressure. My operation wasn't built for that type of shit yet. Me and Coup could've recruited and got some more niggas to work alongside Sergio's men if that's what we agreed to with these new shipments. But the mothafucka never mentioned a gotdamn word about that. How were we supposed to be responsible for some weight we never fucking got or even had eyes on. It was some straight bullshit.

All I could do was get word out and fucking fast. Reach out to all the mothafuckas I'd built a relationship with this past year since I'd been out from North and South Carolina all the way out to Charlotte. In hopes that some shit got back to me on what the fuck happened.

I went ahead and got out of my ride. Told Bruce Lee and the other lil' nigga that we needed to get word out that there was a missing shipment. Not to tie our operation to it but let it be known we were looking for information and would pay. Telling them that any nigga with information that was legit got 10 bands flat out. And if it led to us getting the weight back then they'd get a straight cut from the shit off top before distribution. It would still be a loss, but we had to put some bait out there to get at least one nigga in the streets to tell us something.

I left them to get to it. While they were already making calls. Now me and Coup wouldn't use the phone. None of the niggas we did business with used phones when it came to real shit. Sergio only called my burner that was prepaid and used for a single shipment at a time before I copped a new one.

I needed to get up with Coup and make some moves right fucking now. It didn't make senses that two big ass trucks up and disappeared. The whole thing was off. Even Sergio calling my line about it like he did. I headed out to the farm and tried calling Coup again. Still with no fucking answer. This nigga had me worried on top of the other bullshit. I sent a "911" text alerting him that some serious shit was going on. If that didn't get a response than I'd know some shit was up for real.

About halfway to the spot while I was driving North on the highway, Imani called.

"Bae, you got to get to the hospital right now!" She sounded frantic."

"What's up?" I was on high alert. Already expecting it to be some shit with Coup.

"Brandi and Coup been here all night. The baby is HERE!!! I'm an auntie. So hurry yo' ass up and get up here!" She all but screamed into the phone.

A sigh of fucking relief ran through me. "Oh, okay. I'm on the way."

After our conversation, now en route to the hospital which was about a 20 minute ride in good traffic, I couldn't help getting right back to business. This was gonna fuck up Coup's day when all he should be doing was fucking celebrating becoming a new father. I hated to have to bring him this shit. But at he end of the day as long as we didn't have any fucking answers or any product, Sergio would be on our ass. And we didn't want those type of problems.

We were nowhere near the size or status we needed to be to ward off cartel shit. So like it or not, right now we were at his fucking mercy. But I didn't like that taste in my mouth one bit. It was all fucked up and one thing about a nigga like me, I didn't like dealing with a mothafucka that tried to strong arm me. Respect was given as long as it was receieved. I wasn't feeling his attitude on some bullshit that really didn't have shit to do with our team.

Imani

When I say this little girl was a straight angel I meant that shit. She was so beautiful even as a preemie newborn when a lot of baby's honestly needed a day or two to get their coloring right, she was already perfect. I knew it might be because I was bias and this was my niece. But I didn't care. Even Amyra was extra excited to get to see the baby. Like she already planned on all the ways to play with her.

Amyra finally laid down on the window seat. I put a blanket over her so she'd take a nap. Falling asleep right with the tablet in her arms. She hadn't even gotten to see King yet and I knew when she did she would be bouncing off the walls again with excitement. So while she slept I relaxed and held my new niece some more.

Not surprisingly, Coup was already acting overprotective of his daughter and Brandi. I loved to see the shit. He even snapped at the nurse when she came in to check if Brandi needed help to soothe the baby's crying. The poor nurse didn't know what to do. She jumped in her damn shoes, almost started crying herself and turned back around. Needless to say nobody else came in and bothered the couple or any of us for that matter. Even though I knew we really weren't supposed to be staying in here like this for so long. I'm sure it was against hospital policy or some shit.

"Damn bro, you didn't have to scare that poor nurse like that."

"Nah, sis she should know better. You don't bother a new mother like that. And she damn sure isn't 'bout to touch my daughter. I didn't like her energy anyway."

"Ohhh Lord..." I exaggerated and laughed.

Brandi didn't say nothing. I knew she was tired as hell. I'd been there done that and still remembered the feelings like yesterday. Brandi was with me the whole time. Demont's sorry ass missed Amyra's birth and finally showed up the next day before I was released. Always on some bullshit for real. I don't know how I'd ever put up with his shit. I guess that was the old me, because it couldn't have been me now a days. I felt like a whole new woman.

Demont was out of the picture anyway. And out of mind. His ass took off and never came back around and he wasn't missed by me or MY daughter that was for sure. His ass could stay gone for all I cared.

Khalil walked into the room, and my eyes instantly were glued to him. Damn near drooling like he didn't just do my body right and leave me satisfied and asleep from the good dick. I wanted more and I couldn't even front. If there wasn't a room full of people and we weren't here at the birth of our niece than I would gladly jump on him and get some more. No matter how sore he had my pussy.

"Hey bae" I walked over to him.

He held onto my waist, naturally wrapping his arm around me in his protective way. And of course I felt the electricity when our bodies touched. Like always. The spark never left.

But he didn't say anything and the stiffness in his body told me before he said a single word that something was wrong. But he played shit off.

"Congrats B. And bruh! This some big G shit."

He went closer to the bed and looked down at the baby sleeping peacefully in Brandi's arms. It really felt like a close knit family. A twinge of sadness came over me thinking about how we lost our child. But maybe we could try again. I had to keep faith. At this point with how things switched up in the blink of the eye and we were back together now, who knew what would happen next.

After graduation, and starting my own business, I did want to build a family with Khalil of our own. Not that he treated Amyra like she was anything but his. But I wanted to give him what we lost.

Khalil was smiling and looked across the room where I had walked over to. By the window to check on Amyra while he said his congratulations. Our eyes locked and it was like we were inside each other's minds thinking the same thing. Of course I didn't know for sure, but it was a feeling.

"I got a couple cigars down in the car to celebrate nigga. Let's go take a ride for a minute."

Yup some shit was up. Me and Brandi exchanged looks and Coup's demeanor changed. It was still a happy and light-hearted but more serious now. His guard went up just like how Khalil came in. Now the others picked up on what I felt from the jump.

Coup leaned down kissed his daughter and then Brandi on the forehead. Slid his hand over top of her head and then started walking out of the hospital room behind King.

When Khalil opened the door, he was met with 4 officers pushing their way into the room. Immediately him and Coup put their hands in the air, kept calm. But pissed the fuck off. Mad as hell that 12 showed up at the damn hospital. It couldn't be anything but bad news and some serious charges.

"Aye, let go of me. Let us go out in the hallway and ya'll mothafuckas can do what you came for."

"Leave my fucking family out of it." Coup added, ready to talk shit and kill one of these pigs.

King reached back with his hand, "Chill bruh." Then turned back around facing the first officer who walked up in the room. Who was smiling all smug.

I knew it was taking everything in Khalil and Coup not to go off. But all that would do was upset the kids and cause these fucking cops to charge them with resisting. The same shit they wished would happen. So I was proud of how our men were handling the situation because it was some straight bullshit. The whole damn thing.

"Actually, we're not here for either of you. Not this time Mr..... Oh right... King. Is that right?" He chuckled. He brushed past Coup and King with the other 2 police with him. The second one walked towards me pulling out handcuffs.

I knew they were here for me now. It was the shit from the hotel. I knew it might happen, but in this moment with everything happening I was angry as hell. Caught off guard.

"This is some bullshit." Was all I could say.

But then the door opened again, and none other than the fucking the devil himself, Marcus walked in. He was dressed in regular jeans and a T-shirt, but sure enough the nigga had a badge hanging around his neck from a silver chain

"Mothafucka!!!!......." King yelled out and charged at Marcus.

Police or not, hospital or not, I knew he was a man first and a street nigga at that. He wasn't about to let the man who violated me get by without a fight. All hell broke loose. King started swinging back to back. He got two good blows in. And at the same time the little ass cop who had cuffs out started pulling my arms behind me back. With everything going on, I struggled against his hold.

"Get the fuck off of me!" I shouted.

Turning my attention back to Khalil who was now on the floor, with Marcus's shoe on his neck literally. Blood coming out of his mouth. While the other fucking office handcuffed him. And the 3rd one held his gun up to Coup's forehead. While he stood in front of Brandi and his newborn daughter. It was like a bad ass dream. A scene from a movie and the shit was happening in my real fucking life.

Marcus, called for backup into his walkie. Then dragged Khalil up to his feet. Khalil looked back at me and nodded. I knew he was telling me to keep my head up and that I'd be good. I felt comforted. So when the bitch ass cop who was holding me started pulling me forward towards the door, I didn't fight or object. The cuffs digging in my wrists.

"Mommy!!!!"

Amyra's scared voice rang out and she ran over to me. Wrapped her arms around my legs holding on as tight as she could. Tears started pouring down my face. The police who was pointing his gun at Coup turned and trained it on my daughter.

"NO. I'm going." I said.

I looked down at my daughter who was balling her eyes out the same way I was. "It's okay baby. Everything's okay. Just a misunderstanding. No worries. Now go over to Auntie B and Coup. You're staying with them and your new baby cousin tonight."

I looked away and turned straight ahead. Kept my head high and started walking towards the door. With her little hands still trying to hold on. Luckily Coup came over to her and picked her up. Took her over to the bedside and held her while she screamed for me to come back.

And that shit broke my heart. I knew nothing would ever be the same for any of us again.

To be continued...

--A Street King's Dream 2—

Hood Series
Hood Love and Loyalty 1
Hood Love and Loyalty 2
Hood Love and Loyalty 3

Gansta Love Series
A Gangsta's Pledge 1
A Gangsta's Pledge 2
A Gangsta's Pledge 3
A Gangsta's Pledge 4

Street Dreams Series
A Street King's Dream 1
A Street King's Dream 2

Summer Heat Series:
(Stand Alones)
Summer Heat Harlem